# THROUGH OTHER EYES

# THROUGH OTHER EYES

## BEVERLEY K. S. FENTON

Library of Congress Control Number:
2002091019

ISBN-13: **978-0971871212**
ISBN-10: **0971871213**


First printing          2002
Second printing         2012


Reprinted in the U.S.A by
CreateSpace

*This volume is dedicated to my three children – Emani, Evan and Emma – who make all this worth it.*

# Table of Contents:

## ACKNOWLEDGEMENTS

This work would be incomplete without these acknowledgements. Many people assisted in several ways and it would be remiss of me if I failed to name them individually and say heartfelt thanks.

First, I give praise, honor and thanksgiving to God who gave me the inspiration and the talent to write these stories. I love you, Lord. Thanks for being my Father, my strength, my Adonai Jehovah, my Jehovah Elohim, my everything.

Without their foreknowledge, a number of pastors contributed considerably to my understanding of the original stories and the times in which the characters lived. They also assisted me with ensuring the Biblical and historical accuracy that was necessary for these fictional renderings of existing Bible stories. They fielded my questions and returned insightful answers which brought clarity to my understanding of the Scriptures. Thank you very much, Rev. Ronald Dewberry, Pastor James Swanson and Mr. Anderson White.

No good book is complete without good editorial services. For this collection, I had the invaluable services of Clauristine

Bramble, Elcia Daniel, Rosenny Fenton and Mavis Small-Abednego. Your keen eyes and pertinent suggestions are appreciated immensely. I thank you all.

It is difficult for an author to get that first work read and commented upon. A number of pastors took the time out of their busy schedules, without hesitation, and provided endorsements. To Dr. J. A. George Irish, Bishop Glen Prospere, Pastor James Swanson and Rev. Moreland Williams, I say a heartfelt thank you. I truly appreciate your thoughtful comments.

To you all, I say, "Thank you and may the blessings of the Lord be with you and yours always."

# *SPECIAL DELIVERY*

*Coincidence.     Oh, no!     It is no coincidence that I was a part of the life of one of the greatest Israelites ever to be born. All of Egypt should be honored that his birth took place within its borders.  To some, my role may appear small and insignificant.  But anyone who has borne a child that has died at birth due to the ineptitude of the midwife knows that I played a very important role in, not just his life, but the life, the existence, the history of our people.  I delivered him from within his mother: safely.  This was a special delivery.*

◆          ◆          ◆

My grandmother had been a midwife.  In fact, so had her grandmother and countless women in our family for generations. Little did she know, when she decided to train me to succeed her, that she was setting in motion a chain of events that would be recorded forever in the annals of history. Neither of us, however, would ever be remembered as a part of the official narrative.  That is all right though because she also taught me something else: an unshakeable belief in the God of Creation who rewards openly the deeds done in secret. It is that belief that allowed me to have a part in this narration without the need to hang my head in shame.

Many years before my birth, Jacob and his household arrived in Egypt. I was born in Egypt, but I had heard the tales of God sending Joseph ahead to make provision for us for the day when the famine would envelope our land. To some, it may seem that it was a rough way to make provision (at least, for Joseph), but that is how God works: in ways that we do not always understand. There is no doubt, however, that God had made provision because we came here and we prospered in numbers and in possessions. This was all well and good for a time, but soon, a Pharaoh who felt that this could not be allowed to continue ascended the throne. He looked at the sheer numbers of Israelites, contentedly making an honest life, and began to see visions of us rising up against him and biting the very hand that had fed us to the greatness that we were enjoying in Egypt. *Evil thinks as evil would do.* He began to imagine us – ungrateful wretches that he believed that we would be – joining with his enemy in times of war and fighting against the Egyptians. *Ingratitude thinks as ingratitude would do.* This imagined threat drove Pharaoh to a madness that few have ever witnessed or are willing to admit exists. It is a madness that seethes beneath the surface of an individual's consciousness with its deadly flames flaring high in the sky, going unnoticed because of the cloak of invisibility lent to it by its stealth mode, to the detriment and destruction of that individual's enemies. In this case, it begat a hellish plot of genocide. Pharaoh was not satisfied to banish the people of Israel from within the borders of Egypt as he had originally thought. Instead, he plotted to eradicate us from off the face of the earth.

Initially, Pharaoh established a method of slavery that was designed to so physically wear us out that we would be unable to multiply. He possibly felt that we would die quicker than we could reproduce. He set taskmasters over us who were charged not only to work us mercilessly but also to afflict us physically. Even while we were busy building Pharaoh's treasure cities of Pithom and Raamses, the taskmasters' whips knew no rest.

In spite of the cruel treatment that became our daily fare, we continued to multiply. This frustrated Pharaoh to no end. It seemed to him that our ranks swelled to spite him. It was a personal affront. How dared the Israelites? Did we not know that he, the great Pharaoh, had determined that we would dwindle into nonexistence? In his insanity, he did not doubt for one minute that he could ensure that this did in fact happen. He commissioned his taskmasters to work us harder, oppress us more. This had no effect. His eyes did not glaze over and roll back in his head as may have happened with the normally insane. He did not throw fits that had him rolling about on the ground, foaming at the mouth and gnashing his teeth, in danger of swallowing his tongue. This insanity of the soul only led him to think of other ways to ensure that his decree bore the desired fruit.

This Pharaoh was a far cry from his ancestor who had welcomed us, Joseph's relatives, to Egypt. He was very different from the Pharaoh whom Jacob had blessed on his arrival in Egypt. The only similarity seemed to be the title that they bore. There was no resemblance in their characters. As our numbers continued to grow, Pharaoh ordered that we serve with even greater rigor. Most of us were only allowed to work outdoors, at the mercy of the elements. We worked with brick and mortar or in the field. Yet, our numbers grew. There had to be some reason why his plan was not working, Pharaoh thought. These descendants of Jacob had to be receiving help from somewhere. Sure, we were: our God. This did not occur to Pharaoh, though. He began to think that the taskmasters were not doing their job as they should and a few of them were put to death as an example to the others of the seriousness of their commission to afflict the Israelites. This, however, did not stop the explosion of our numbers.

Finally, in desperation, Pharaoh summoned Shiphrah, the other Israelite midwife, and me. Till then, I had no clue what had been going on. Too often, we notice things, but fail to give them a second thought when they do not affect us directly. True, I had noticed that life had changed for many of my relatives, but I had not guessed that this had been at the orders of Pharaoh. I should have guessed this, though. Such injustices as the taskmasters committed against us could not have continued if they were against the wishes of Pharaoh.

My commission filled me with horror.

"When you do the office of midwife to the Hebrew women, if it is a boy, kill it. If it is a girl, you can let it live."

***What?!!***

The horrific nature of the order so stunned me that I wished that this, my first trip to the palace of Pharaoh, had never taken place. I would gladly have gone to my grave without seeing the inside of these walls. Every memory of my visit to the royal residence will be infested with the maggots of Pharaoh's request that I become a mass murderer. We had so few midwifes as it was and so many babies were being born. Now, Pharaoh was demanding this.

I had barely glanced sideways at Shiphrah when Pharaoh had issued his orders, but her reaction had seemed much the same as mine.

My thoughts spiraled about inside my head like rags being tossed about on the winds of a storm. I was scarcely able to take in Pharaoh's monologue.

*. . . turn against us in times of war . . . control the numbers . . . all up to you two . . . protect the land for our children . . . kill the boys . . . an order . . . taskmasters killed for failure to obey. . . kill the boys . .*

*. kill the boys . . . kill the boys . . . kill the boys.*

I must have been able to acknowledge the order of Pharaoh in a manner that did not betray my feelings as we were soon outside the suffocating walls of the palace and on our way home. Neither of us dared to speak of what had just taken place. It was as if not speaking about it would make the order vanish. I never did find out how Shiphrah felt, but, for me, it was a surreal experience.

*How could Pharaoh ask us to do this? What kind of people did he think that we were? There is no way that I can do this. It goes against all of the things that I learnt at my grandmother's knee about the sacred duty of the midwife. Of greater significance is the way that it contradicts all that my belief in Jehovah dictates.*

Just as I did not discuss Pharaoh's commission with Shiphrah, I dared not mention it to anyone else. Pharaoh had made sure to warn us that if we breathed a word of his instructions to anyone, he would kill our entire families. First, he would have our children drowned before our eyes and then, he would have our parents killed in front of us. What more persuasion did we need to remain silent?

For me, just thinking about his instructions would have been deterrent enough since they left me with a tainted feeling. It was as if I had committed some grave sin. I went about my duties as if nothing had happened: at least, that is how I made it appear on the outside. I tended to my family responsibilities as usual and I was extra careful when delivering a baby. It seemed not only that there were more of them since I had received my new charge, but also that there was a definite increase in the number of boys. I could not carry out Pharaoh's wishes and I knew that it would not be long before I was again summoned to his presence. I could only hope that he would want to caution me again before he had me put to death for failing to carry out his orders.

Soon, Pharaoh summoned me again.

"What is going on? Did I not tell you that you are to kill all of the Israelite boys that you deliver?"

"You most certainly did, Pharaoh, but the women are very lively. Before I get to them, they are delivered of the child. There is nothing for me to do then, but to cut the umbilical cord, make sure that the baby is well and see to it that the mother is not in danger of hemorrhaging. There are even times when the woman has already cut the cord herself when I get there."

"You need, therefore, to get to the women with greater haste."

"Respectfully, I am getting there with as great haste as usual. It is as if the babies themselves are seeing to it that they arrive safely. Labor seems to have been shortened. There is nothing that I can do if the baby is already born when I get there."

"I understand your predicament if what you are telling me is the truth. It may just be that you do not want to carry out your orders. If I find that to be the case . . . It seems that I have to think of some other method of controlling the numbers. Continue to try to get to the women before the babies are born so that you can kill the boys. If that fails, I have another plan."

With that, I was dismissed. I breathed a sigh of relief. I knew that I had to spend many a season in prayer for forgiveness for the lie that I had just told Pharaoh. It was going to take many an unblemished kid's sacrifice to atone for that lie. But, I felt that I had had to tell it. The labor was no shorter than usual. I just could not kill the babies. I wondered what new horror Pharaoh had in store for us. He had said that he had another plan and I knew that, whatever this plan was, it was bound to be worse than the one for Shiphrah and me to kill the baby boys. I shuddered at the thought of this yet unknown plan of his.

It was not long before the veil was removed from Pharaoh's new plan.

"We have come to verify that the baby that you just gave birth to is a boy!" bellowed Pharaoh's soldier.

"Why?" whimpered the mother. She had just given birth to a healthy and robust baby boy. Fear was written all over her face and I was sure that my face mirrored the same emotion.

I knew not how they had discovered that an Israelite woman had just given birth, but I knew that this was just the opening scene of the play, "Let's Eradicate The Israelites III." I felt nothing but revulsion mixed with anger and fear for the soldier and his boss at that moment. How could they seek to deprive a woman of her precious baby at this time? I did not know what exactly they planned to do with the baby, but I did know that the mother would never see him alive again.

The mother began to mutter to herself it seemed. I recognized what she was doing. She was not merely muttering to herself.

She was praying. She prayed as she knew that only the God whom she served could reverse what was about to happen.

While she muttered with her eyes closed and her arms firmly around the precious bundle that I had recently handed to her, the soldier stepped closer to her. He snatched the baby from her and unwrapped its blanket. A cry of anguish escaped from the lips of the mother. I could barely look at the soldier. I was sure that the hatred that I felt for him at that moment would burn holes through his chest, his head or whatever part of his anatomy my glare fell upon. I reined in my anger and asked a question that I regretted having asked when the answer came. I was gored by the eviscerating effect that the answer had on the recently delivered mother. "What are you going to do with him?"

"Our orders from Pharaoh are: 'Every son that is born ye shall cast into the river and every daughter ye shall save alive.'"

*What?????*

The question shrieked through my brain, but the woman's scream prevented me from uttering it. I fell to my knees at her side to comfort her while one soldier tramped off with her son in his arms.

"We will report to Pharaoh that you were the midwife who delivered this baby," said the other soldier.

It had not dawned on me before that Pharaoh would be interested in knowing who had delivered the baby if it was male and alive when his minions put in their appearance to do his diabolic bidding. It was foolish of me not to have given any thought to that.

"You got here as soon as I had finished tending to the mother. What did you expect me to do? Leave her to bleed to death while I made my report to Pharaoh?"

"It is not for me to decide what you ought to have done. My instructions were simply to have the child destroyed if it is a male and yet alive, and to report which of the midwives had delivered it."

As he turned to leave, I said, "You do your duty and I will do mine."

The whimper that escaped from the distraught mother brought my thoughts back to her. I knew that anything that I could think of doing for her now would be ineffectual, but I had to make some attempt to comfort her. I took her in my arms and rocked her while I crooned to her as if she was a baby. As many hymns as I knew, neither words nor tune of any came to mind.  Not that any hymn would be truly appropriate at this juncture. Eventually, a tune did come to mind and I hummed it while I rocked her, hoping that this would bring her some solace.  It seemed to work as, mercifully, she was soon asleep.  I eased her back on to her pillows and went in search of the old lady who had been with her when I got to her home.  It was her turn to tend to the needs of her daughter.  It was better her than me to have this impossible task: mending the broken heart of a mother whose child had been ripped from her arms to feed the insanity of a crazed man.

I had to drag my heart home from there. I should have asked them for some rope to tie around it, so heavy was the load.  It took many a bruise as it bumped over the "what-ifs" and "how-can-hes" that dotted the path between their home and mine.  I felt useless.  There was nothing that I could do to put an end to this madness.  A cloud shrouded my steps back home and the weight of the depravity of what I had just witnessed sat upon my shoulders. *How could anyone in his right mind visit such torture upon the innocent?*  The worst part of it, in my mind, was that this was just the beginning.  Pharaoh was not about to end this here. He was not simply making an example of this one baby. I would have to witness many more Israelite women in similar anguish and, again, I would be helpless to either prevent their pain or to diminish it.

The days came and went. I delivered several babies and the sound of the tramping approach of Pharaoh's men seemed to become a part of the ritual: labor, delivery, cut the umbilical cord, in come the soldiers, give them the baby, watch the mother die inside, go home. Had it been a musical performance, it seemed that that would have been the crescendo that gave the piece life and meaning. Soon, it became the norm. That did not make it any easier for the mother to accept. That did not make it any easier for me to deal with. But, it became the norm nonetheless. Pharaoh was leaving nothing to chance. Even stillborn boys were taken away and their bodies tossed into the river.

One night, however, Pharaoh's soldiers failed him. I was called to the home of a Levite, a priest. His wife was about to give birth. They already had a daughter, Miriam, and I sensed that this woman was hoping to have a son in spite of the danger of doing that in these times. I prayed that she could get her heart's desire, but I knew that this was a sure way to heartache. In a very short time, the baby arrived. It was a boy. I cut the umbilical cord and, out of habit, listened for the tramp announcing the arrival of the soldiers of death. I heard nothing. I handed the baby to his mother, hoping that her time with the baby would be sweet though I knew that sorrow lay just around the corner. Still no arriving soldiers. I wondered how this was possible, but I almost held my breath while the mother looked at her son, seemingly in awe. Her love and joy made her face radiant and my heart break because I knew that this would be short-lived. I stopped just short of commenting that the soldiers were taking a long time to get here. I hated to spoil her joy. Eventually, she looked up at me.

"Look at him," she said. "Isn't he a beautiful child? I know that we should declare his birth to Pharaoh, but I cannot bear to part with him so soon. Allow me to hide him here for a while and then I will let my husband take him to Pharaoh himself. Just allow us a little time with him. If we are asked, we will not say that you delivered him. I promise you. Please allow us to keep him for a little while."

Her pleading eyes and the tears that glistened there did more to me than her speech or any other eloquent oration could have done. I saw there an unconditional love. I could not turn this woman's baby over to Pharaoh any more than I could have killed it as he had instructed me to.

"The secret of the birth of your baby is safe with me. I thought that Pharaoh's men would have come for him by now, but they have not. I will leave now and when they get here, you can tell them that you delivered him yourself, if they find him. If they do not come, when you turn him over to Pharaoh, if you turn him over to Pharaoh, is up to you. If anyone asks me about your baby, I will tell them that when I got here, your baby was already delivered and it was not alive."

*I am going to need my own herd of unblemished young animals before this is over. So many lies to atone for.*

The Levite's wife looked up at me with the gratitude that flowed freely from her heart overflowing from her eyes.

"Thank you. May Jehovah bless you for this kindness that you tonight show to me and my family."

"There is no need for you to thank me. Thank Jehovah for He has shown you great mercy. Pharaoh's men still are not here. It does not even seem as if they are coming."

I left the home of this Levite, priest of the people of Israel, and his wife, baffled.

*How is it that Pharaoh's men had not put in their usual appearance? What is different about this baby? Was Pharaoh setting me up? Did he want to see if I was not going to report the birth of this Israelite boy?*

Strangely, no one asked about the baby that I had gone to deliver that night. That made it easier for me to atone for the lies that I was prepared to tell. The days went by and I heard nothing of the baby and Pharaoh's men did not come to take me away.

Three months later, I heard that when Pharaoh's daughter had gone to the river to bathe, she had found a baby in an ark made of bulrushes. The story said that she had fallen in love with the handsome little boy and could not bear to have him put to death in accordance with her father's decree. Instead, the story continued, she had hired an Israelite woman to nurse the child for her. I wondered if this was the same baby. I suspected that it was. I hoped that it was, but I dared not ask for any details. I could not allow anyone to say that I had demonstrated any interest in that baby as I was sure that Pharaoh was wondering how that one had managed to slip through his net of genocide.

◆          ◆          ◆

Many years have passed since then. I am no longer delivering babies. In fact, I am no longer able to deliver anything but the air that I inhale and exhale and that just barely. I am an old lady living with her daughter, thankful for the kindness that it is shown me daily by my offspring and their offspring. I thank God that He has spared my life to see all the days that I have seen. Many around me say that we are now living in turbulent times, times filled with sin and hardship like never the world has seen before. I tell them that each generation is faced with sin in one form or another. I am not saying that these are easy times because it seems that this Moses, Pharaoh's Israelite grandson, was really sent by God to ensure that our people get released from the bondage that Pharaoh has imposed upon us for so many years. When I hear of the wonders that he and his brother Aaron have done in Pharaoh's presence and yet Pharaoh will not release the Israelite people, I thank Jehovah that the remainder of my days on this earth are few because I know that things are going to get worse for the Egyptian people before they get better. The water turning to blood, the frogs all over the land, gnats . . . What next?

As I close my eyes and prepare to draw my last breath, I think of that strange night when I assisted that Levite woman to give birth to the son whose name now makes so much of Egypt tremble. I think of her pleading with me for her son's life. Little did she know that we preserved him for such a task as this: to secure the release of our people from the tyranny of Pharaoh.

With my last breath, I thank Jehovah that I, Puah, unsung heroine that I will be, had the privilege of being a part of a very special delivery: the delivery of Moses, a divinely chosen deliverer of our people.

# PRODIGAL

The house was well lit and voices emanated from what should have been a quiet house.

*Has something happened to my father? I could not stand to lose him. He is all that I have.*

I hastened closer with my heart pounding an uneven staccato rhythm in my chest. As I neared the house, in spite of the fear that was clogging my every pore and causing my every sense to malfunction, I realized that nothing was amiss. The voices were raised in gaiety: a sure sign that the misfortune that I had imagined had not befallen me. The sounds, which so clearly spoke of merriment and rejoicing, caused me to sigh with relief. Fast upon the heels of that sigh rose the cloud of puzzlement. I could hear the musicians providing the sounds of joy and, through the windows and in the yard, I could now see the figures of people dancing. *Why? What is the cause of this merriment?*

I drew closer to the house with a haste that belied the tiredness that I felt after a long, hard day in the fields. As I came through the gate, I saw one of my father's servants hastening by with a jug that was used to keep wine cool during a celebration.

"Joseph," I called. The confusion that I felt in my heart was obviously written all over my face. I did not have to ask him what was going on.

"Master Peter, your brother has returned home!" he said with a delight that bathed him in a glow that harked back to Moses when he came down from Mount Sinai. "Your father had the fatted calf killed to celebrate his return . . . "

Instantaneously, the joy that surged from Joseph was sapped from him. My rage had jumped out and choked it. That glow-inducing joy now lay at our feet, a miserable picture of its former self. In its place, a thick awkwardness stood between us. I had said nothing, but the look of thunder that had clouded my features told Joseph all that he needed to know. He realized that he had been gushing to the wrong person. He did not know why, but one thing was clear to him: something about this celebration did not please me. The longer he looked at me, the more unsure he became of himself. It was obvious that I was displeased. He feared that the messenger was about to suffer for the message. He suddenly remembered the mission that I had stopped him from.

"I, I, I have to take this to your f-f-father," he stuttered as he moved off, embarrassed.

He was embarrassed and I was ashamed. I was ashamed because my anger was so palpable that I could not conceal it from a servant. By morning, all of the servants would be talking about the fact that I was angry that my father was throwing a party in honor of my brother's return. They would be saying that I wished that he had not returned. They would say that and shake their heads and they would not be far wrong. After all of the pain that he had caused my father, I did wish that he had stayed where he was. I wondered what had brought him back here.

♦       ♦       ♦

"Don't you ever feel tired of the life that we live here with Father, Peter? Every day is the spitting image of the day before. I am bored to death of this place. I must leave here  soon or I will shrivel up and die."

"What are you saying, Luke? We have a good life. We do not know what it is to be hungry. We have clothes on our backs and a roof over our heads. Besides, we have a father who loves us very much and provides for us very well. What craziness has gotten into you?"

"Peter, are you satisfied to be a country yokel, working from sun up to sun down for Father? Is that all of the ambition and imagination that you have? There is a great big world out there with much more to offer than this. I need to go out there and taste and see those pleasures. I know that it has to be better there than it is here and I know that I can make it if I go off to see the world."

"Luke, you must be crazy! What are you going to do when you go out there? How are you going to sustain yourself? Do you expect Father to support you while you are out there *tasting and seeing*?

"Yes and no. I will ask Father for my portion of his wealth. I will take that with me and that is how I will sustain myself."

"Do you expect that this will be enough money to keep you going for the rest of your life?"

"No, but I will find some means of making the money multiply. I do not know how I will do that yet, but I am absolutely sure that this life here is not for me."

"Where exactly do you propose to go? Where are you going to live when you get there?"

"I do not have an answer to either of those questions. When I get on the road, I will go wherever it takes me."

"Luke, have you gone absolutely crazy? Are you listening to yourself? You have no idea where you are going or why, but you know that you are leaving here. My brother, a plan like yours will lead to sure ruin. I beg you to stay at home and think about this some more."

"I have thought about it. I have been thinking about it for a long time and there is nothing else for me to do, but to speak with Father, get my share of his wealth and be out of here."

"I see that you have given this much thought. Destination: unknown. Where you will live when you get there: unknown. Means of support there: also unknown. I hope that when you go to Father with this ill-thought-out scheme of yours that he is able to talk you out of it because I am clearly not getting through to you."

"Peter, you have always been too conservative and determined to do exactly what Father expects of you with no sign of an original thought. Well, that life is not for me. I would die from the absence of excitement here. Every day is a replica of the one before it and the one before that. I must go. I only wish that if you are not coming with me you would wish me God's blessings as I go."

"Luke, I wish that you would not go. But if you do go, I do wish you God's blessings. He knows that you are going to need it to protect you from yourself."

"Some day, Peter, you will see that I was right. Here comes Father. I will go and speak with him now."

Peter left to complete his chores and Luke greeted their approaching father.

"Father, I was planning to come in search of you. I need to speak with you about a matter that has been on my mind for some time now."

"What is it, my son?"

"Father, I need to get out and see the world. I need to know what lies outside of the confines of the life that we have here. I want you to give me my share of your wealth so that I can go off to make a life for myself away from here."

Their father's eyes grew as round as chariot wheels for a brief moment. His shock was soon replaced with a deep sadness.

"Why, son?"

"Father, don't you ever tire of the monotony of your life here?"

"No, son. I do not find it monotonous. Each day, I have a different task to attend to and, even tasks that need to be done every day do not seem monotonous as some new twist always seems to arise to make it interesting."

"Why sit here and wait for something new 'to arise', Father? Why not go out and make it happen?"

"Son, life is not about endless days of pleasure and new experiences. We often need to repeat the familiar in order to learn the lessons that the Heavenly Father has sewn into them for us."

"Yeah, repetition in order to learn the lessons," sneered the son. "It will not take me a lifetime to learn the lessons that are here, on these premises, for me. In fact, I dare say that I have learnt them all already."

"Son, you are young and the young have restless spirits, but that does not mean that you should flee the safety of the sanctuary that I am able to provide for you to go out and get traumatized by the world. The world is a very cruel place with none of the safety that you take for granted here."

"Who said that we must always be safe? Can't it be that there are lessons for us in facing danger alone and overcoming it."

The bugle call of Luke's impatience sounded in his father's ears. In an attempt to quieten this, the father decided to give Luke an opportunity to gush about his plans.

*That should make him less impatient with me. People always love a chance to speak of their plans for the future.*

"Son, where are you planning to go to?"

"I do not know. I figured that I would first go wherever the road takes me. From there, I could always move on if I do not like it."

The father desperately tried not to show his alarm.

*OK, so he does not know where, but he must have some idea of how he is going to support himself.*

"Son, how are you going to support yourself when you get to your destination?"

"I am not sure about that either, Father. It depends on the opportunities that present themselves when I get to where I am going. I will have the money from you and I will have to make that the basis of my income."

"But, Son, you must have some idea. Will you own animals? Will you buy a vineyard? What?"

"Father, I told you that I do not know. What more do you want me to tell you?"

The lack of a plan really alarmed the father.

*I cannot allow him to go off into the world like this. When you do not know where you are going, any road can get you there and the roads out in the world are thorny. He is bound to get hurt. Father God, show me how to direct my son.*

"Luke, I beg you to take some time to consider this some more and then we can talk about it again. In fact, take a year to think about it and, if at the end of that time, you still feel that you must go, I will give you your portion of my wealth and let you go."

"A year?"

Steam was almost coming through Luke's ears. He stared at his father for a while. His anger stood between them as alive as they both were. His father looked at the rage and wished that there was something that he could do to make Luke realize that his were words of wisdom. He feared that Luke would leave without the money that he had initially asked for.

"Is six months better, then, Son?"

"Six months is an awfully long time, but I see what you are doing. You are hoping that I will change my mind. It will not work, though. To prove it to you, I will agree to six months."

With that, they parted. The father hoped that Luke would grow out of this obsession in the next six months. He knew that he was certainly going to pray hard that Luke did. Luke, on the other hand, hoped that his father would not spend the next six months, trying to dissuade him from leaving.

The six months passed without incident. Luke continued to fantasize about getting out into the world and being his own man. Occasionally, he even gave thought to where he would go and how he would support himself there. He found that he was getting no closer to an answer to either of these questions, but this did not perturb him in the least. He knew that these things would take care of themselves when he got out there. The most important thing was that he got out there.

In the meantime, the father was praying for Luke to change his mind.

*Dear God, the one who knows the hearts of men and what makes us who we are, I lay my son, Luke, before you. You see his desire to go out into the world with no plan for his own survival. Father, I beg you to look in mercy upon us both. Him because he is so blind to the dangers that he is embracing and me because I do not know how to dissuade him without pushing him further away. At this time, O God, I ask you to show him the folly of his plan so that when the six months that we agreed upon is at its end, he will no longer desire to go off in this manner. Amen.*

Each day, the father prayed. While they consciously avoided the subject, he was sure that Luke had not given up the idea. As the six months grew closer to its end, he began to despair, yet he continued to pray that the Lord would show Luke the way. The father knew that if Luke's mind did not change, he had no choice. He would have to make the division of his assets and send Luke on his way.

Six months later to the day, Luke approached his father again.

"Father, six months have passed. I still want to go away from here to see what the world has to offer and make a life out there."

The pain that showed in his father's eyes made Luke almost wish that he could change his mind. He regretted causing his father such pain, but he knew that he had to go. He had to see what lay away from here.

"OK, my son, a deal is a deal. I will give to you the share of my wealth that would come to you. Tell me, though, where are you going to?"

"Father, I no more know that now than when we spoke about it six months ago, but when I get there, I will send you word of my whereabouts."

The father's heart sank further within him.

*Why, God? Why didn't you answer my prayer?*

With a heavy heart, the father made the division. Scarcely had Luke received his portion than he was off. He packed his stuff and left with a haste that brought more pain to his father.

*Is it really that bad for them here? Peter seems to be content to stay here, though. Dear Lord, please look over Luke wherever he goes.*

Luke soon forgot his promise to let his father know where he was and what he was doing. He got to the city and he spent his money with no regard for the next day. He was having a great time. He never lacked for companions. Life was one long party.

*How could Father have thought that there would have been danger here?*

Eventually, Luke realized that his money was finished.

*Already? How could that be?*

Worse yet, a famine arose where he was. Many days, he was hungry. This was partly because he was no longer able to afford to buy food and partly because his friends had suddenly disappeared. There was no one around to give him a meal. After a few days of this, he had an idea: *I'll get a job.*

Finding a job was not as easy as he had thought. Some weeks passed before he found one, feeding swine for one of the nearby farmers. He did this for a while. Often, he had to eat some of the husks that were provided for the swine. One day, as he shared lunch with the swine, he realized the desperate nature of his situation and he thought of the life that he had once enjoyed at his father's house. He thought of the depths to which he had sunk.

*How many of my father's servants have enough food to eat and to spare while I am eating what is provided for the pigs? I will go back and ask my father for a job on his compound. I will tell him that I know that I am not worthy to be considered a son, but I would be glad to serve him as a servant.*

Immediately, Luke got up and set off on the journey home. It seemed, as he walked along, that a burden was being lifted from his shoulders. He was no longer going to perish from hunger. He realized that he would no longer be equal to his brother, but the life of one of his father's servants was surely better than the life that he had been enduring.

◆          ◆          ◆

Father was no longer the same man that he had been prior to Luke's departure. While he was careful to hide how he really felt from me, I knew that he was a broken man. His son had gone off into the world with nothing but his pockets full of money. He had no plan and that was a certain path to ruin. He had promised to send word of his whereabouts and he had not: a sure sign that he had nothing good to report. I watched my father age despite his determination to appear as if he had no cares in the world outside of the day-to-day worries of taking care of the homestead. Soon, he was a shell of his former self. That irked me. I hated Luke for what he had done to our father.

Then, Father got the surprise of his life. He saw Luke in the distance.

Are my eyes deceiving me? He is much thinner and he is dressed in really tattered clothes, but that person looks a lot like my Luke. Can it be? Can it really be him?

He was so overjoyed that he ran forward to meet him. The closer he got, the more evident it became that it was indeed Luke. When he got to him, he hugged and kissed him.

His prayers had been answered. His son had returned. Tears gushed from his eyes.

"Thank you, Lord!!! Thank you!!!!!" he shouted with his hands held up towards Heaven.

"Luke, you are home. My prayers have been answered. Let me look at you."

He held his son away from him and looked at him for a long time.

"You are thinner than you were before, but that will change with time. I am just so glad to have you back. Let us go to the house. I wish that your brother was already back from the fields so that he could see you."

"Father, I have sinned against Heaven and in your sight and I am no longer worthy to be called your son."

"Nonsense, boy."

By then, they were within the compound and one of the father's servants was nearby.

"Bring forth the best robe and put it on him. Put a ring on his finger. Put shoes on his feet."

To another, he shouted: "Kill the fatted calf. We must eat and be merry. My son whom I thought was dead is alive. He was lost, but he has been found!"

The servants hastened to do their master's bidding. They had little time to gossip about this thing that was happening, but they knew that there would be time to discuss this at length in the days to come.

Soon, the compound was ablaze with the sounds of merriment. The fatted calf was being roasted and my father's invited guests had arrived to share in his joy.

♦          ♦          ♦

"Son, what is going on? Why have you not come inside to share in the celebration of your brother's return?"

Joseph must have told him that he had spoken to me outside some time ago.

The anger that I felt stood solidly between my father and me, thicker than the wall that surrounded the compound. He did not understand why I was so angry, but he knew that it was up to him to fix that and he had to do so quickly.

"Come on, Peter. Your brother has come home. Let us make merry."

"Father, all of these years, I have worked here for you. I have tried never to do anything contrary to your wishes and you have never once given me a kid to have a party with my friends. But, now that Luke is back, you kill the fatted calf and throw a party. Luke, the one who left you to squander your wealth in the company of harlots and other undesirables. I am sorry, but I cannot be merry at his return."

Father was saddened by my response. It was true. I had worked for him faithfully. I was the model son who asked for nothing in return. At no time had he given me an animal to have a party with my friends.

He had never thought it necessary. I had never complained, but now I was angry and Father had to realize that it was justifiably so. But, he looked at me as 'Peter, his Peter, who was not going anywhere'. He thought that all that he had was mine so I had no need of a party to celebrate my presence. So, he felt that he needed to explain to me why a celebration in honor of Luke's return was necessary.

"Peter, my son, all that you say is the truth. Your brother Luke did go off and squander his inheritance and, long after we are all dead, whenever people speak of us, he will be referred to as 'the prodigal son'. You, on the other hand, Son, have always been with me. All that I have now is yours. But, it is fitting that we should celebrate the return of your wayward brother. We had thought that he was dead, but we know now that he is alive. We had thought that he was lost, but he is found. Do not let anger consume you. If you cannot find it in your heart to forgive Luke, you will have proved yourself no different to him."

"Me, no different to Luke? How could you say such a thing, Father? Now, I know that I definitely cannot come inside. Maybe you wish that I had left. Maybe I should leave now to make room for your beloved who has returned."

"That is not what I am saying, Peter. I may have seemed to take you for granted and I am sorry about that. But, Luke needs our forgiveness and our assurance that we are prepared to accept him back into our family. Do you expect me to tell him to return to where he is coming from? Do you want me to tell him that he can come back home, but he is now less of my son than you are? No. Luke knows what he has done. He will not forget that he had left us, foolishly. But, now that he is back, it is up to us to welcome him back with more than words. We have to embrace him with love. Come on in and join me in celebrating."

"Celebrate? What is there to celebrate? If things had been good with your beloved Luke, you would never have seen him again! Now, you expect me to celebrate that he is here! How long is he here for? Until he can get you to give him some more money? How could you let him use you like this, Father? Well, I will not be taken in. Celebrate all that you like, but I will have no part of it!"

With that I stormed away. I could not believe that my father was so gullible. He watched me stomp away and I knew that he was deeply grieved by my choice, but I could not be part of this farce. I could not pretend to be glad that Luke was back.

♦               ♦               ♦

The father shook his head. It took all of the effort that he could muster not to shed the tears that burned behind his eyes. This grief was heavier than any that he had ever borne before, even that that he had borne while Luke was away. Much as he had tried to be a good father and supply all of the needs of both of his sons, he had produced two prodigals. One was wasteful of his material possessions. The other recklessly wasted his love, protection, guidance and all of the lessons about compassion and forgiveness that he had taught to them both. Which of his sons was more worthy of the title "prodigal"? Neither. They were both prodigals in their own way. He felt that he had failed them. He must commit himself to fixing that. But, tomorrow, he would begin. Today, he had much to be thankful for and he was going to celebrate.

With that thought, he returned to the party, hoping that he would be able to salvage one son before he began the task of restoring the other, more subtly so, prodigal son.

# *THE HANDMAID*

"Hell hath no fury like a woman scorned." So say the sage among us.

I, however, have observed that, "Life hath no fury like a barren woman!"

They had been married for years, more years than some of us, their slaves, had been alive. Yet, they had no children. She was barren. They, more kindly, say that Jehovah had shut up her womb. I did not consider that to be a kinder way of putting it. It might be a more genteel way of describing it, but it certainly was not kinder. It opened the field for speculations about what she and/or her parents had done to invite Jehovah's wrath to the extent that the payment was 'a shut womb'. That cannot be kinder. Suffice it to say, she was barren. She was seventy-five years old and she had no children. She was barren.

But you know that all married women, particularly women of power and influence, have the answer to every problem. She was no exception. She was *resourceful*. You know that that is the way that the story will be told. She looked around and saw all that her husband possessed and knew that only one thing was missing: an heir. That reflected badly upon her. If things were not tidy about the compound, that reflected upon one of us. If the crops failed to flourish as expected, that reflected upon one of us. If the animals were sick and dying, one of us was failing to perform our duties as we should. No heir. That reflected upon her. Any woman who was worth anything would be able to provide her husband with many sons and she had failed to provide even one daughter. Her husband had not been critical, but she could not bear the looks of other women and, it is alleged, she felt that her husband was getting that beaten look in his eyes. He could not understand what he had done why Jehovah had not blessed him with children. After all, hadn't Jehovah actually promised that he would be the father of a great nation? The apparent failure of Jehovah to make good on His promise ate through all of her gentility and the wisdom of advanced age like a canker, and revealed an arrogant "*I can fix anything*" attitude. No one would previously have accused our mistress of having such a character, but there it was.

Don't get me wrong. They were great masters. We were well provided for. I liked it here, but the treatment that my friend received at the hands of a couple whom she was obliged to serve was reprehensible. At least, that was how it seemed to my feeble, human eyes. I'll tell you the story and you tell me what you think.

♦          ♦          ♦

It was not uncommon for wealthy men to buy slaves from varying parts of the country or even from other countries. In fact, some places were known for producing better slaves for certain tasks. (You know that the slave traders propagated such stories to drive up the price. Rich men fell for them not because they were duped, but because they could not afford to seem not to be taken in by the story. Anyone who was anyone got his or her slaves to perform that task from that place. It was a sort of snobbery, but it worked to the advantage of some.)

These were hard times. Parents were selling their children into slavery in order to be able to provide for the ones whom they kept at home. Some people were really that poor. That was how two of my friends and I became the slaves of this couple.

We all worked around the home. We were domestic slaves. Mary was a cook. I was a washerwoman. My other friend, Hagar, was the personal slave of the mistress. She was called her handmaid. Here we were, far away from home, but we had each other. Life was not easy, but we had clothes on our backs, food in our stomachs and a roof over our heads. It was not our roof. We could not leave it to our children, but it was a roof nonetheless and we were not about to be put out of it. We tried to work hard, giving our master an honest day's work. It was not too bad here. Yes, some days, our mistress was really miserable, but who does not have an off day? OK, some people's off days came more often than others', but what else do you expect? The poor woman had no children while everyone else seemed to be popping them out without a thought. My friend said that she liked working as the mistress' handmaid although the mistress was often testy and exacting. In fact, my friend felt somewhat sorry for her. I guess I was sorry for her too. What is life with no children?

Then, one day, my friend came to Mary and me, all excited. She told us that she would not be sharing sleeping quarters with me anymore. She did not know why, but the mistress was allowing her to have her own quarters. Mary and I were a bit wary of this sudden good fortune. After all, we had been in Canaan for ten years now and we had always shared the same quarters. Why had the mistress suddenly decided that Hagar needed her own quarters? Mary had only moved from the quarters that we were sharing when she had been allowed to marry Benjamin. I was due to move to different quarters soon, but that was only because Daniel and I were to be married. The mistress knew that Hagar was about to have the quarters to herself. Why move her to new quarters now? Something was terribly wrong here.

"What have you done for her lately?" I asked.

"Girl, you had better look this gift horse in the mouth," muttered Mary.

"Believe it or not, if it seems too good to be true, it **IS** too good to be true. There is a catch," I added.

"No. The mistress is a decent person. She likes that I help her a lot and this is her way of showing her gratitude," responded Hagar.

"Gratitude?" I asked. "Girl, her husband has already paid for you. You have to do whatever she asks you to. Where is the room for gratitude in your relationship? You have to be grateful that she does not, on a whim, decide to have you killed. I know that you have to accept these quarters, but there is more to this than she is telling you."

We talked and talked. Hagar thought that she had got lucky, but we knew that there was more to this sudden largesse than met the eye. Mary and I did not know what was brewing, but we were sure that our mistress was not suddenly struck by the good job that Hagar was doing. We could only hope that she was not about to lose her life.

The next day, as I was placing some clothes on the rocks to bleach, I saw Hagar rushing by. I called to her and she stopped and spoke to me. Something was different. Her eyes never met mine. I asked her if all was well with her and she assured me that it was. She even smiled a very short-lived smile. Her manner spoke volumes in contradiction to her words, but I could not imagine what was the matter. I even asked her about her new quarters. She said that they were fine and she liked them. I could not accurately put my finger on how much of what she said was not the truth, but I knew that some of it was not and that bothered me. I was bothered by the fact that she felt it necessary to lie to me. We had been through so much together in the past. I was bothered by the fact that something was the matter with her. I was very upset so when she cut our conversation short abruptly and hurried away, I did not attempt to stop her. I was too worried. Something was terribly amiss here.

As soon as I could, I found Mary to discuss this strange set of events with her. She had been looking for me. She said that she had seen Hagar and her encounter with her had been much like mine. We were both very worried. That night, we tried to think of what could be the matter with her, but nothing that we came up with seemed like a reason for her to lie to us. It was as if she was afraid of something.

The next day, I was hoping that I would not see Hagar. I usually saw her everyday, but I was hoping that today would be different. I knew that it was a vain hope, but I was still hoping. I saw her and it was a repeat of the day before: eyes on the ground, monosyllabic answers and the "nothing is the matter" mantra. She was almost sour. Mary and I began to get very concerned. It went on like that for weeks.

She would not admit that anything was the matter. I had not yet decided how I would deal with this new person that she seemed to be. It got to the point that my heart fell when I saw her coming my way. I would take a deep breath and follow her lead. Imagine my surprise when the old Hagar returned. One day, just like that, she was her old self: laughing and smiling, looking me straight in the eye and as chatty as ever. Was I losing my mind? Maybe it had been my imagination. Were Mary and I both delusional? I think not. She definitely had been different yesterday and for many days before that. I decided to take it slow. I needed to see if the old Hagar remained with us or if the new one put in an appearance the next day.

The next day, the old Hagar was still with us. I was pleased. I wondered what had brought about the change. I decided to take the bull by the horns and ask her.

"Hagar, what had been the matter with you? You had been acting pretty strangely for a while."

Her eyes fell to the ground for a brief moment and mixed emotions played across her face before she answered.

"I know that both you and Mary are due an explanation. You have been such patient friends, but I did not know how to tell you this."

"What could you have done that is so terrible that you could not share it with us? That is what friends are for: to share through thick and thin."

"I . . . the . . . You remember the new quarters?"

My heart fell and I felt a little unsteady on my feet. I feared the worst, though I did not know what that would be.

"The master comes to me at night."

My heart hit the sole of my feet with a resounding thud, bounced back up to mid calf and then flapped about on the inside of the sole of my foot like a fish that had just been taken out of water. Eventually, it settled on the sole of my foot like a dead weight.

*No! NO!! NO!!! NO!!! NO!!!*
*NO!!!! NO!!!!!*
*NO!!!!!!*

The scream inside my head grew to a crescendo. I was not sure if I had actually screamed aloud. I looked around and no one seemed to be paying attention to us, so I guessed that I had not. That was the catch: the mistress had given Hagar to her husband. Her hope was that Hagar would produce an heir for her. If her intention had been for her husband to take Hagar as his wife that would have been done before he started coming to her at night. It was all about Hagar producing an heir for them, not for Hagar.

"Do you understand what this means?"

"Of course. He likes me."

"Don't be silly, girl. You are the handmaid of the man's barren wife."

"I know. She thinks that it is okay. In fact, it was her idea."

"Of course, it was her idea. He would not have set you up in your own quarters right under her nose if it were not. It is her way of giving him the son that he wants and she cannot provide."

"What is so wrong with me giving him a son? He wants one really badly."

"He wants one. She wants him to have one and when you give him one, they'll take your child from you and he'll be their son."

"No, that will not happen. He would not let her do that."

"Yeah! He could not stop her if that is what she wants to do."

"Well, we will just have to see about that. I hope that I do give him a son. He is such a nice man."

"Give him a son and he will be a nice man that you used to know. If you are lucky, they will sell you to someone in this country. You'll see your son passing by, once in a while."

"I tell you that that will not happen."

With that, she left in a huff. I was so sorry for my poor, deluded friend. She was thoroughly taken in by this man's wife-sanctioned attentions. Poor Hagar!

That night, I told Mary about my conversation with Hagar. She said that she had previously heard something to that effect, but she would not believe it and that is why she had not told me what she had heard. She had thought that it was vicious rumor. I was really disturbed.

I became more troubled when Hagar began to distance herself from Mary and me. She was always in too much of a hurry to really talk. Our conversations were very few and very short. They were never the free, open interchanges that they used to be. Whatever we learnt from her was public information and, even then, it was like pulling teeth to learn that. I was really saddened because I knew that Hagar did not understand what she had got into.

Then, I heard that Hagar was pregnant. I heard it from another one of the washer girls. I could hardly wait until I saw Mary to ask her if she had heard the news. She said that she had, but she had not seen Hagar. We decided that the first chance that we got, we would ask her directly if it was the truth.

The opportunity presented itself that afternoon. I was taking up some dry clothes when I saw Hagar approaching. She was walking with that super-upright bearing combined with a swagger that she had recently acquired. I hated her walk just because I knew that it was saying, "I am a cut above you plebs. I am the master's mistress." Nonetheless, I called to her jovially and she condescended to stop and speak with me. I knew that I had to cut right to the chase.

"How are you doing, Hagar? I heard that you are pregnant. Is that so?"

"Well, good news travels fast," she gushed.

"Good news?! Girl, you just don't get it, do you?! There is no good news in that. You are being used."

"No, I am not. We are so happy that I am pregnant."

"We??!"

"Yes. Abram and me."

"Abram and me," I sang back to her. "Do you hear yourself? Hagar, wake up, girl. There is no 'Abram and me' as you put it. It is Master Abram and Mistress Sarai getting another service from their slave girl. Your feelings do not figure into this picture. They only give you the impression that they do to keep your spirits up and to make you compliant. You know that pregnant women need to be in good spirits."

"Well, you are doing a lot to keep my spirits up, aren't you?'

That slap stung. I knew that to her, it seemed like I could say nothing good about her 'good fortune', but I knew that there was no good in this fortune for her. If only I could communicate that to her.

"I am sorry, Hagar, but I wish that you would see that you are just being used."

"I know that you do not understand, but Abram and I have an understanding. It is only a formality that we are not really married. Soon, though I am sure that we will make that right. You will see that all is well."

My eyes jumped out of my head and stopped a hair's breadth short of her face. At least, that is how it felt to me, but I guess that it had not actually happened as Hagar seemed unfazed by my reaction. Of course, her lack of response could be an effect of the drug that she had taken. That must be some powerful bush tea that she has been drinking. I do not know what she had been drinking and/or inhaling, but whatever it was, that baby was in serious danger of being brain damaged like its mother obviously was. . . . *Abram and I have an understanding . . . It is only a formality that we are not married . . !!!!!*

"You do remember that Master Abram has a wife: Mistress Sarai. What about her? Is she just going to sit back and accept her handmaid becoming her equal? After all, if he marries you, you will suddenly be her equal."

"Sarai has no say in the matter. What is she going to do anyway? Men take new wives all the time. What use is she as a wife anyway? She is barren. Sarai will just have to live with it."

I was on the verge of fainting. In fact, for a while there, I was not sure that I had not done so. I looked her deep in the eye and saw that she was as serious as leprosy.

She meant what she was saying. *My poor deluded friend!* ' *Abram and I have an understanding. . . . Sarai will just have to live with it. . . .* ' The audacity of referring to them in that manner. Familiarity really does breed contempt. She did not even know that **they** had an understanding. Her only part in it was to understand that she was to do what they required of her. *My poor deluded friend!*

With that she left, leaving me with my one repetitive thought: *My poor deluded friend!*

It was a good thing that she had left because I did not know what else to say to her. *My poor deluded friend!* I must have looked like the crazy person that my friend had become because I felt as if my hair was standing on end. *My poor deluded friend!* Every pore was wide open as a result of the shock of what Hagar had been saying. *My poor deluded friend!* My nostrils were flaring. My eyes were in danger of never getting back into their sockets. Even my ears stood askew. They felt like the large flapping appendages of an elephant. It is cruel to subject your ears to the rantings of one as deranged as my friend had obviously become. *My poor deluded friend!*

I spoke to Mary later that day and told her of my conversation with Hagar. She was amazed, but, mostly, she was really hurt. She had known Hagar longer than I had. Tears trickled on to her cheeks as we spoke.

"Why are they using her like this?"

"Don't worry, Mary. We will pray that Jehovah will see Hagar through this with as little pain as possible. Maybe, she is right and we are wrong."

"Yeah, right," was Mary's response. She knew that I was just trying to comfort her.

In a few days, everyone on the compound knew that Hagar was pregnant. It was all that most people could talk about. Each time I heard mention of it, I felt sicker and sicker.

At first, Hagar seemed to enjoy being the bearer of the heir. She had a glow. I guess she was entitled to that. She was pregnant by the master and everyone else had to respect the status that that elevated her to. She was all around the compound with airs and graces that she had not had before. Some of the other slaves found her to be really obnoxious. She made demands of them that she would not previously have. I thought that I ought to speak to her (even though she had not been speaking to me recently). I had no success. On the occasions that I tried speaking her, she was quite brusque and her manner clearly said, "Leave me alone, plebian." She did not deign me worthy of her notice now.

As the months went by, there was a lot of talk about Hagar. Yes, the compound was buzzing with the fact that she was the one who was providing Master Abram with a child, but I also heard stories of her being disrespectful to Mistress Sarai. Apparently, she was calling her "Sarai" to her face and refusing to do some of the things that she was told to do. What had gotten into this girl?

I wondered how long this situation would continue. After all, Hagar was Mistress Sarai's slave girl. She was not Master Abram's wife.

Then, one day, I was summoned to Mistress Sarai.

Hagar had disappeared.

"Do you know where your friend Hagar has gone to?" she asked.

"No, Mistress. I do not. I have not seen her for a few days. How long has she been missing?" I asked. *Not that I would tell you even if I knew.*

"No one has seen her since last night. Are you sure that she did not tell you of a plan to go somewhere?"

"I am sure, Mistress. She passed me by the bleaching stones two days ago. She had a heavy trough on her head. I do not know what she was carrying or where she was going since she did not speak to me."

I recalled then that it had struck me recently that Hagar was not looking as well as she had or should. She had seemed to be tired and drawn, but I had put it down to the wear and tear of pregnancy. It had also seemed that she was given many hard and unusual tasks like that heavy trough that she had been carrying the last time that I saw her. On some days, she had been seen outside doing backbreaking work in the hot sun. We wondered if Master Abram wanted her to lose her baby. Had he just wanted to prove that he could impregnate a woman? *You could never tell. Rich men are strange creatures.*

"Return to your duties," was Mistress Sarai's terse dismissal.

As I left her, I began to worry. Something was amiss. Hagar was missing. Why had she left? Where had she gone? Was she all right? I was greatly perturbed by her unexplained absence.

The next few days were some of the longest that I had ever lived through. Mary and I kept each other informed of any news that we heard about Hagar during her absence. Even Benjamin and Daniel, kept abreast of the news about her disappearance. They knew that it was important to us. Just as suddenly as she was gone, one day, she was suddenly back.

I was hanging out clothes and she was passing by.

"Hagar, you are back!"

I could not hide my joy even if I had wanted to. The other washerwomen looked at me strangely when I exclaimed at her appearance.

"Where were you? How could you just leave us like that? Not even a word to Mary or me. Why did you leave?"

She looked at me and I saw none of the "soon-to-be mistress of all I survey" attitude that had characterized her manner recently. On the contrary, she seemed so meek. I could not believe it. The old Hagar seemed to have returned. I did not know what to make of it.

"Let us walk aside a bit," was all she said.

As soon as we were out of earshot of the other washerwomen, she continued.

"I was leaving this place for good. I wanted to take myself and my baby away from that cruel woman, Sarai. She was oppressing me too much. It isn't my fault that she is barren. I could not bear any more torture at her hands. 'Hagar, I want this. Hagar, I want that. Hagar, comb my hair. Hagar, cut my toenails. Hagar, make me tea. Hagar, take out my bathwater. Hagar, take these clothes to the washerwomen. Hagar, lift this. Hagar, move that.' And not a word from Abram to stop her. Girl, men can be so weak. You would think that Abram would tell her that she cannot treat me like that. She never did until I got pregnant."

*Oh, so it is Mistress Sarai who wants her to lose the baby. That figures. Poor lady. It must be terrible to have to live with the fact that you are barren and even worse when your handmaid is having a child for your husband.*

"Yes, and you never called her Sarai before you got pregnant either. Do you think that it is fair to say that the pregnancy has changed you both?"

"OK, that is true," she offered reluctantly. Then, after a moment's reflective pause, she added, "I despise her. But, she has proven herself to be a despicable woman. Abram and me was her idea. What did she expect? Does she think that all women are barren like she is or was she secretly harboring the hope that the fault was really Abram's. Look at my condition and she works me like a dog. . ."

"Why don't you appeal to Master Abram if you think that she is treating you so harshly?"

"Who him? Girl, earth hath no punishment like being pregnant by a spineless married man."

I was shocked by her new vision of Master Abram. In fact, so shocked that I did not know what to say. I quickly drew the conversation back to my original queries that had gone unanswered.

"Where were you, Hagar?"

"I only got as far as a fountain on the way to Shur when I was met by an angel of the Lord who sent me back."

"Angel of the Lord? Yeah. I believe that."

"You don't have to believe me, but I know that if I had not been met by him, I would not have come back here. He urged me to return to Mistress Sarai. He was even able to tell me that my baby is a boy and that I should call him Ishmael as the Lord had heard my affliction."

"OK. You have had your fun. Now, tell me what really happened."

"That is what happened. I am not kidding you. He also told me that my seed would be numbered to the extent that it is beyond reckoning."

I looked at my friend. This confirmed my previous suspicions of insanity. *I had met an angel of the Lord . . . I should call him Ishmael . . . my seed would be numbered . . . My poor deluded friend! I do not know what our owners had done to her, but she has really lost it this time. Shame, she used to be such a nice girl.*

In a few months, the baby arrived. Master Abram had a son: Ishmael.

*OK, so she had got Master Abram to call the boy Ishmael. That did not prove anything. She is my friend, but she is crazy.*

♦           ♦           ♦

Time really waits for no one. It seemed as if one day, Ishmael was born and the next, he was thirteen years old.

Just about that time, Master Abram claimed that he had an encounter with Jehovah and he now knew Him by a new name: El Shaddai. El Elyon, God, Jehovah, Adonai Jehovah, El Shaddai. It seems to me that it really does not matter what you choose to call Him since the name is only an attempt to describe His character and capture His sovereignty, holiness and power. Anyway, the Supreme Being had now revealed himself to Master Abram as El Shaddai, the strengthener and satisfier of His people. As a result of this meeting, there were a few changes to be made. Master Abram was now to be called 'Master Abraham' and Mistress Sarai was now 'Mistress Sarah'. In addition, he said that he had been instructed by El Shaddai to be circumcised and to circumcise all of the males in his household – slaves, freemen, everyone. After this, all males were to be circumcised at eight days old. We did not quite understand what this was about, but it was not in our place to understand. It was simply in our place to submit.

No one who heard about this new trend seemed to think that Master Abram, sorry Master Abraham, had lost his mind this time. You see, the claim, all about the land, was that Master Abram, Master Abraham, was a man close to Jehovah's heart. I take that with a few grains of salt (actually more than a few), but that is the claim. To be truthful, if it had not been for his awful treatment of Hagar, I would have had no problem believing it to be true. You would have to be in close with Jehovah to be able to defeat King Amraphel and his allies with 318 men as Master Abraham had and only take a blessing from Melchizedek, a priest, in return for your kindness.

One night, a few months later, Mary came to my quarters.

"My friend, this news could not wait until tomorrow morning. Mistress Sarah is pregnant."

"Yes, Mary and the building of the tower of Babel was a roaring success not to mention that Cain and Abel are living in perfect harmony somewhere just east of here."

"I am serious. I am not kidding."

"Girl, I cannot believe that some rumor monger could have you running about the compound in the night, bearing tales."

"This is no tale. It is the truth. I got it from
. . ."

"Mary, I do not want to know who you heard with this ridiculous tale. Do you know that Mistress Sarah is eighty-nine years old? Girl, I was born in the night, but not tonight."

"OK, don't believe me. You'll see."

We talked for a few more minutes about other things and then Mary left.

The next day, I heard some of the other washerwomen talking about the same thing: Mistress Sarah was pregnant. Almost simultaneously, Hagar came across the yard.

*Banished handmaid walking. As soon as her child is here, Ishmael and his mother will have to go. I do not know how Mistress Sarah will be able to pull that one off, but I do know that she is not going to want her child having to compete with Ishmael for their father's affections. Oh, no!*

"Hi, Hagar."

"Hi. I guess that you too have heard that the barren one is now, miraculously, going to have a child."

She got straight to the point. No tiptoeing around the issue like an Egyptian walking on hot sand. Her hatred for the mistress dripped from every pore. No one could blame her for feeling the way that she did.  Mistress Sarah had oppressed her mercilessly for the last fourteen years.  It was as if she felt compelled to show Hagar that she may be the mother of Master Abraham's only child, but she – Mistress Sarah – was still his wife and Hagar's mistress.

"Yes.  I heard."

"If I had thought her unbearable before, I know that she definitely will be obnoxious now.  I will no longer have something that she does not have unless her child is a girl.  If only Abraham and I had had more children."

"Do you really think that that would change anything?  After all, he is married to her."

"Yes, but that would have been moot if she had no offspring.  If her child is a girl, Ishmael will still be the heir.  I know that I have taken enough abuse at her hands.  Ishmael ought to reap some reward from it.  I am only here because of him."

*Amen!  But I cannot tell her that.*

"Do not fret.  Master Abraham will see to it that both children get what is rightfully theirs.  He will take care of Ishmael even though Mistress Sarah has a child."

"I appreciate your faith in Abraham, but you do not know him like I do.  Sarah is the one who runs the show in that marriage. If she were to tell him to kill Ishmael so that her child has no competition for his affections, my son would be just my lovely memory."

"Don't think such dark thoughts. It cannot be that bad."

*Yes, it can and most likely is.*

"Yes, it is. You'll see," she said, dejection written clearly all across her face.

*I really do not want to see that. Girl, you had better take your son and head for the road. He'll be away from his father, but you'll both be alive. How can I tell her what I am really thinking?*

At that point, one of the young girls who worked around the household came running up.

"Hagar, the mistress is calling for you."

"Tell her that I'll be there."

"You had better go and take care of her needs."

"Let her wait. She only wants another opportunity to show me that she is in charge. I know that she is my mistress, but she does not have to spend all day every day devising ways to show that."

"Go to her, Hagar. You do not want to be punished again."

"She has given up on the usual forms of punishment as she sees that she can afflict my body, but she has ceased to affect my mind. Anyway, I would not want to get you into trouble, so I'll see you again soon, my friend."

With that, she left. She was not hurrying though. I was sorry for my friend. Master Abraham and Mistress Sarah had used and abused her down through the years. Everyone knew that Mistress Sarah regretted the arrival of Ishmael and wished that both he and his mother were far away from here, but there was no way that she could get Master Abraham to send his beloved Ishmael away. After all, he was his only child. But, that was about to change and my friend was upset. Hagar was not being as paranoid as I had let on. Her fears were real, but I could not tell her that. It would only intensify her worry. She would lose her leverage if Mistress Sarah had a boy. Considering the way in which Mistress Sarah had treated Hagar ever since she had conceived Ishmael, it was not unlikely that Mistress Sarah would ask for Hagar's head (and maybe even Ishmael's) on a platter if Mistress Sarah's child was a boy.

*Jehovah, have mercy on my friend. Let Mistress Sarah either have a girl or change her attitude to Hagar and Ishmael so that all will be well with them.*

The time of Mistress Sarah's confinement arrived. She gave birth to a boy. They called him Isaac. Though we were obliged to appear to be happy for our master, I was very sad. I was sad because I knew that harder times were ahead for Ishmael and his mother. On the eighth day, Isaac was circumcised as had become the practice here.

As soon as Isaac was weaned, Master Abraham threw a party to celebrate. If I could have dared to not attend, I would have. My heart was so heavy. At one point, I noticed that Ishmael seemed to be laughing. Kids are so easily amused. His demeanor seemed like more than just happy amusement though. I became concerned when I felt that Mistress Sarah had also seen him. I knew that that would mean trouble. I was distressed because I knew that it took very little to get him in trouble with his father's wife.

The next day, I saw Ishmael on the compound and I felt a small sense of relief. Maybe, Mistress Sarah had not seen what I thought that I had seen. A few days passed and Hagar and Ishmael were still around, so I began to take comfort in the thought that it was my imagination. Ishmael had just been enjoying a good joke and Mistress Sarah had not noticed his laughter.

Alas, I was wrong. I got out into the yard one day not long after the party and the other washerwomen were abuzz with the news: Hagar and Ishmael were gone.

"Gone? Where?"

As the story unfolded, Mistress Sarah had seen Ishmael laughing on the day of the celebration for Isaac. She concluded that he was mocking. After all, Isaac was a second son. That was Mistress Sarah's conclusion. No one had any knowledge of Ishmael having said that. Anyway, Mistress Sarah had pestered her husband to get rid of Hagar and Ishmael. She had apparently said that she did not want Ishmael to be joint heir with her son. *I guess that mothers do have a keen sixth sense.* Master Abraham, just as Hagar had said was weak because he gave in to his wife's request. He had got up early that morning, given Hagar bread and a skin of water and sent her on her way.

Bread and a skin of water? He might have spat on them before he had them beheaded. Such good that bread and a skin of water would do them. His kindness must have overwhelmed Hagar. She must have run to him and kissed his feet while tears of joy ran down her face. She must have felt set for life. I know that I am overwhelmed. (*Don't flare nostrils.*) I had begun to see Master Abraham through different eyes and I know now that he has allowed his wife . . . No, he has joined his wife in treating Hagar most unfairly. It is despicable what these people have done! I wonder if he is thinking that one day, after he and his wife are dead, Isaac can make this up to Ishmael and they will live happily ever after. That, however, would be the dream of the foolish. Ishmael and Isaac could never be friends after this. I do not even think that their descendants will be able to get beyond this. It will take many generations to rise above this. It is not impossible that they will ever get beyond it, but highly unlikely. Generations of hatred spawned by the gutless actions of a man who was afraid of his wife. No doubt, his major concern was to live in peace with his wife. Of course, if he is to speak about this, he is going to have some story about the Lord telling him to let them go. Well, if ever my girl Hagar needed to meet an angel of the Lord it is now.

◆          ◆          ◆

I never saw Hagar again. I heard that she was living in Paran. I heard that that was where she and Ishmael ended up after his weak-willed father on the urging of his jealous stepmother summarily dismissed them. Things must have worked out for them. He became an archer, I heard. I also heard that Ishmael married an Egyptian girl. Hagar must be proud. He married a girl from home.

◆          ◆          ◆

So, you have heard Hagar's story. Do you now agree that the fury of a barren woman is unparalleled?

# BEHIND THE LINE OF SCARLET THREAD

"What are they doing? We know that they are still out there. We have heard them moving about for six days now. We have heard their trumpet blowing. It seems that they have been going around the city wall for their sounds have faded and then returned. What are they trying to do: kill us with the weaponry of nervous anticipation of annihilation? If they are going to attack us, why don't they go ahead and get it over with? Are they hoping that our fear of them will kill us before they get in here?"

"I do not know, but I do know that I am not even going to peep out in the hope of catching a glimpse of what is going on. I am sure that once I am in here, I am safe, regardless of what is happening out there. You will also be safe if you remain in here. I cannot say the same if you venture out to investigate their plan."

"Is that so? How can you be so sure?"

"You are going to have to trust me that I am sure."

"Trust you?"

I did not allow my oldest sister's husband to go any further. I jumped right back in.

"Yes, that is what I said. Just as I said when I urged you to come here: you have to trust me. But, if you do not want to, feel free to return to your homes. Once you go though, you are on your own. And, no, you will not be free to come running back here."

"Trust you, you say," said my oldest brother. "What makes you an authority on what will keep us safe? How is it that you have the inside track? Why did we have to come to your house? Why won't you just be honest with us? There has to be more to this than you are telling us."

The unasked asked more than the uttered words. It was not the tone. It was *the look*. *The look* that never failed to speak volumes. That look said it all: *You must have entertained some Israelite soldiers in exchange for this favor.* That look was in the eyes of all of my relatives who were beginning to go stir crazy, tired of being confined in such close quarters. I know *the look*. I know it well. I had had to develop an immunity to that look. It followed me everywhere that I went in Jericho. Even some of the very people who enjoyed the services that I had to offer had the audacity to give me *the look* when they met me in the streets. Hypocrisy is alive and well in Jericho. I can assure anyone of that. What really hurt though is that in this case *the look* was undeserved. I could live with it when it was earned, but now, it really hurt.

"If you doubt me, the bravest among you can go out and come back to tell the others what death feels like!!" I hurled at them.

My eyes moved from one stony, self-righteous face to the next. No one was willing to go out and prove me wrong, but they were all prepared to sit here and give me grief about how I was so lucky as to be able to save them from the edge of the Israelite sword. Truly, hypocrisy is alive and well in Jericho like nowhere else.

I must admit that the waiting was making me begin to wonder what exactly these Israelites had planned for Jericho. It seemed like a mighty unusual form of attack. This was end of the sixth day since we had been able to hear their presence outside our walls. In all this time, the gatekeepers had not dared to open the gates of Jericho. In fact, they had been ordered not to. I only knew that the Israelites were still there because I live on the wall. None of their sounds, at least while they were on this side of the city, failed to reach up to my house.

"We had better try to get some rest now. It is pointless for us to sit up all night, anticipating what tomorrow may bring: more trumpet-blowing or attack."

"Just listen to the Israelite of Jericho. I really would like to know what makes you such an authority on what we should do," sneered my oldest brother.

He really hated the fact that he was not the one with the answers. He could bear having to defer to our father, but me – a lowly, insignificant woman, worse yet, in my line of work – that drove him absolutely crazy.

"You do not have to take my suggestion. You can sit up all night. You are free to do whatever you please and that includes leaving here. I, however, am going to bed. Good night, all!"

With that, I turned on my heel and left them, hypocrites all.

It seemed that I had barely fallen asleep when I was awakened by trumpet blowing. I was tempted to stay in bed a while longer. I was sure that it was just another day of Israelites marching around outside the city wall. But as I lay there, the trumpeting seemed to go on a little longer than usual. *I had better get up and be ready to face whatever the day brings.* I got dressed and joined the rest of my family who seemed to have also realized that today was going to be different. We did not know what it would bring yet, but we sensed that it was different.

The blowing of the trumpets continued for what we eventually realized was seven circuits of the city wall. Then, Jericho as we knew it, fast became a memory. We heard the blood-chilling shout of a multitude and the crash of the wall around our city falling down. The day that we had fearfully anticipated was here. It had thundered in upon us in a manner that we could never have been prepared for. I knew that this was it for our fair city. I hoped that the spies were men of honor. I dared not let any of my terrified relatives see my wavering thoughts. They were searching my face for some assurance that the carnage that we were sure was going on outside would not come to us. I had to at least appear sure that we would be safe. After all, I had lured them here with that promise. Before any of us could speak, the young men whom I had met before when they came to spy out Jericho came crashing through my door.

"We have come to take you and your relatives to safety, Rahab. Make sure that everyone is here. Follow us. Anyone who leaves the group has taken his life into his own hands."

In a few minutes, we were all gathered together. They escorted us out of the city and deposited us outside their camp.

"Remain here," was their brief caution.

Having glimpsed what was going on in Jericho, none of us needed to hear that twice. We huddled together and watched the flames go up as the Israelites set fire to Jericho, our once beloved home. We could hear the screams of death emanating from our compatriots. It was a sobering experience. Sobering to my relatives because they knew that they could have been among the dead. Some of them were even wondering about where they were going to get stuff from to start their life anew. Some were thinking of where they were going to live now that Jericho was no more. Some were having thoughts of doubt about living among the Israelites: *Will they make us their slaves?*

I was amazed by their concerns. Your life had been spared, mysteriously spared, for you had done nothing to deserve it and that is all that you can think of? But, those are my relatives for you: self-centered, unwaveringly sure of their own deservedness.

I knew that I had done nothing to deserve being saved from death. I had lived a sinful life. There are no two ways about that. This God whom the Israelites serve is a mighty God. Not only had He delivered my people and many others into their hands but also He had the ability to spare sinners. After all, here am I. Now, that is some power! That is what made this experience, our escape, so sobering for me. As I reflected on the gift of my spared life, I knew that the time for a change had come. I had thought about it before, but never seriously. I knew now, though, that I needed to know more about this Israelite God for I had to follow Him. He had brought me from behind the line of scarlet thread safely and He deserved my gratitude and reverence.

◆          ◆          ◆

How had I gotten behind the line of scarlet thread in the first place?

If someone had told me that this would happen to me (or even could), I would have laughed them out of Jericho. I had no illusions about who I was. I was Rahab, the harlot. I was not the kind of person who could be singled out for such an honor. I could be singled out for ridicule, even by the very people who singled me out for pleasure. But honor? Be serious! There never has been and I doubt that there ever will be a "Harlot's Awards." After all, most of us in this business do not admit to our line of work and none of our customers admit to being satisfied with the service although they may repeatedly seek us out.

But, to return to the idea of this being an honor. There was no doubt about that. I had heard of the sparing of the Israelites' firstborn because they had placed the blood on their doorposts. The Israelites were a chosen people. The stories of their escape from Egypt and their conquering parade from there to here confirmed that. They had saved the lives of their firstborn by keeping them behind the scarlet mark. I was sure that there was a definite parallel between that and this. I, too, was saved because I remained behind the line of scarlet thread. It was a mind-boggling concept for I knew who I was. I was Rahab, the harlot.

Anyway, the story . . .

It was dusk and two men entered my premises. I took one look at them and knew that they were not from Jericho.

*Who are they?  Coming together?  Before nightfall?  They must be lost!*

They knocked on my ajar door.  I told them to come in and they did.  They claimed that they were on a long journey and needed somewhere to rest before they went any further.

*Yeah!  'Rest' is what they call it now. Okay, I can play along with this game so long as they do not think that they can get two for the price of one here.  I give no freebies.*

It took just a little time before I realized that these men were some of the much-dreaded Israelites.

*What are they doing here? Have I signed my death warrant by having them here on my premises?  Maybe not, they seem harmless enough.  They are much more polite than most of my usual visitors.  I hope that they are indeed harmless or at least mean me no harm.  I had better be extra kind to them.  I do like the feel of being alive.*

I barely had time to get them settled in before some of the king's men came tramping into my compound.

"Bring out those Israelite men who are in there with you!!  They have come to spy out the land!!" they bellowed.

They had to make a show of their authority. No one was to mistake their business with the harlot.

Their bellowing from the street allowed me time to hide the men among the stalks of flax that lay on top of my roof before going out to acknowledge the soldiers.

"Two men did come here earlier, but I did not know where they were from. However, as it got dark, just as the gates were going to be shut, they left. I do not know where they went, but if you pursue them now, you should overtake them."

The soldiers made another show of their departure. No one was to think that they had remained here. They shouted notice of the fact that they were leaving to everyone within earshot as they left.

"You had better be telling us the truth because it will be very unpleasant for you if we have to come here again," one of them bellowed.

"Let's go now. We have to catch those men," another shouted as they turned in pursuit of the elusive Israelite spies.

I waited some time for the city to settle down for the night and for my neighbors to lose interest in me and the activities in my yard that had brought excitement into their otherwise dull lives. Then, I went up to the men on the roof. I was sure that they had heard what had passed between the soldiers and me.

"Listen, I know that your God is going to allow you to conquer Jericho. Your fame has preceded you here. We are all afraid of you. We have heard of how your God dried up the Red Sea so that you could cross over. We heard of the plight of the Amorite kings at your hands. It is obvious that this God whom you serve is God of heaven and earth. I saved you from the sword of the king's soldiers. Now, I am only asking you for one thing: save the lives of me and all of my relatives – my father, my mother, my brothers, my sisters and their families – when you return to conquer Jericho."

"If you do not tell anyone of our plan, if you are killed when we return, we will lose our lives as you lost yours. Once you do not tell anyone, when we come back in the Lord's strength to conquer Jericho, we will deal kindly with you and honor your request."

*Are they for real? Who could I tell that I had lied to the king's soldiers and hid Israelite spies? Do I look suicidal?*

I got some rope and let them down through the window. I know that it is no coincidence that their God directed them to my house. My house adjoined the city wall. Their escape was easy.

As I was helping them to escape, I advised them, "Go to the mountain so that the soldiers cannot find you. Hide there for three days. By then, they will return to Jericho. Then, you can return to your camp."

"Thanks, Rahab. We will keep our end of the bargain. When we come to take Jericho, tie this scarlet rope in this window. Bring your parents, your siblings and their families and your father's entire household here. If anyone goes outside, his blood will be on his own head. On our hands will be the blood of anyone who stays in here and gets killed. However, if you tell anyone about this, we will be free of our promise to you."

*These have to be the crazy ones that the Israelites sent out!! What would I have to gain by telling anyone about our arrangement? I am in no hurry to die. I could at least wait for the Israelite invasion, no need to rush ahead and allow some blabbermouth to see to it that I die at the hand of the king's soldiers.*

"Fine. Let it be as you have said."

With that, they left and I tied the rope (that I had not realized was scarlet until they had mentioned it) in the window, placing myself safely behind the line of scarlet thread.

# A
# DESOLATE
# WOMAN

"No, my brother, do not force me for no such thing ought to be done in Israel. Do not this folly. And where shall I cause my shame to go? And you, you will be looked upon as one of the fools of Israel. Go to our father the king, he will not prevent us from being married."

The look on his face told me that my pleas had fallen on deaf ears. My brother had dropped all pretence of being sick and the real reason for my coming to his house to tend to him without any of his servants present was painfully, sickeningly clear. He was sick in his head with lust for me, his father's daughter. His lust oozed from his pores and the smell of it stank to high heavens.

*"Oh, God of Abraham, Isaac and Jacob, save me from this madness that has overtaken this son of my father."*

♦               ♦               ♦

I was what any parent would want when a baby girl was born: beautiful and sweet natured. I grew more so as the days went by. I lay in my cot, kicked up my royal heels and gurgled. I did not even cry to tell them that I was hungry or wet, I just cooed a little louder. My parents were elated. To the nation, I was my parents' due. After all, wasn't I the daughter and granddaughter of kings? Talmai, my mother's father, was King of Geshur and the Lord God Almighty himself had chosen my father, David. I had often heard the story of how the Lord had sent the prophet Samuel to my grandfather Jesse to anoint my father as king. My uncles all thought that they must have been the chosen one (after all, my father was only a little scrawny young boy), but the Lord had and still has his hand on my father's life.

My brother Absalom always thought of himself as my protector. He was also my mother's son, so, while I did have other brothers, we had a special bond. When we were children, it was better for the wind that it did not blow against my cheeks and cause them to redden as though raw because he got mad. Needless to say, anyone who caused me the slightest distress had earned themselves an enemy for life in the person of my beloved brother Absalom. That is yet to change. In fact, as we got older he got more protective of me. I guess that that is in part due to the fact that I now had a "virtue" for him to protect from the "desperately wicked hearts of men" (as he so often put it).

As I got older, I proved to be not just pretty, but an intelligent girl. Often, my father or some one of the elders would comment on the fact that I had wisdom beyond my years. However, such talk was always followed by a word of caution that I should not allow that to make me forget that I was just a girl. As disparaging as that may sound, I was not offended. I fully understood that wisdom or any knowledge outside of how to command and control my house servants was not necessary to a woman of royal blood. (Not that the men felt that any woman needed wisdom.) I also knew that men desired wives who knew their place, but had the ability to give their husbands good advice that they could pass off as their own ideas among the other men of the kingdom. Absalom had told me all about it. I adored my brother, Absalom. He was everything that I would want my husband to be: loving, kind, protective, caring, wise, a good listener, always ready to teach me, gentle with me yet commanding with the men. He was ruggedly handsome and he loved me like none other ever did and ever will.

I was not in the least bit worried by this "just a girl talk." It was predicted that I would make a good match (that most likely meant a king) and make my parents proud. For generations, kings' wives have been the brains on the throne, but you'll never hear of that from men. Who had told me that? Absalom, of course. My brother, Absalom, saw my ability to reason through difficult and even stressful situations and glowed with pride. It gave him a feeling of intense satisfaction. For him, that meant that if our father (in one of his momentary lapses of lucidity and wisdom) even agreed to give me to a mean man or one who was inclined to treat me unfairly, I would be fine. There were other things that Absalom needed to have known about me, like my ability to reach deep down into the recesses of my soul and forgive, that would have changed the course of history.

◆　　　　　◆　　　　　◆

It was known throughout my father's household that I was kind to the sick and that I had a special touch that made even the sickest well again. The God of our forefathers had blessed me with more than a lovely face. I had a gentle manner and I truly took comfort from seeing the ill get well. I tended to their ailments and I spoke softly to them, coaxing them back to health with words that soothed their spirits. Therefore, no one questioned the fact that Amnon asked our father for me to tend to him when he lay sick.

I made the cakes as Amnon requested, happy with the thought that his appetite was returning. At least, he desired something to eat. He looked on keenly and, as I kneaded the dough and baked the cakes, I spoke to him. I spoke to him of life and all that lay ahead of him. All that he could accomplish as the first-born of King David and eventually as king himself. I spoke of the prosperity in the land and how we were enjoying the blessing of the Lord whom our forefathers had served so faithfully. I spoke of our father and how his subjects thought well of him. I reminded Amnon that one day, he would be thought of in much the same light, but he had to get better first. I even asked him if he thought that I was talking too much. He said that I was not. He enjoyed hearing me speak. The lilt of my voice reminded him that he was mighty lucky to have a sister who could take care of him so well and make him begin to regain his strength, he said. I recalled the story of our father slaying Goliath. I spoke of the prophet Nathan bringing word of the Lord's covenant with our father and the promise of prosperity that that brought to us: his children. (Women were not supposed to know a lot of these things, but my brother Absalom thought that I needed to be knowledgeable.) It seemed not to bother Amnon that I was speaking of things that men would speak of. Foolish and innocent as I was, I never wondered why. I should have had a more questioning mind. Lots of things would have been different then.

Soon, the cakes were ready and I was about to feed my brother. I had to get him better. He was heir to our father's throne. I told him that it was time for him to eat now and then I would tell him more stories of our ancestors until he fell asleep. He agreed and told me to dismiss his servants and tend to him alone. I thought the request sort of strange. After all, it was inappropriate for a young lady to be alone with a young man in his quarters. Amnon must know this. But, since Amnon was making the request, I convinced myself that the fact that we were siblings made some difference to that rule. I made a mental note to ask Absalom about it. Because I was also of the opinion that Amnon's illness was not just physical, but that his brain had also been affected, I obeyed as was proper for a woman to do rather than cause him to sink into a state of further confusion. But no one could have guessed what depravity existed within the walls of Amnon's heart and brain, masquerading as illness.

"Lie with me, my sister."

Time stopped.

*I must be as mentally deficient as I felt that my brother was. He did not say that. I must do much penance for having such a vile thought. It will take at least the blood of an unblemished lamb to appease Jehovah this time.*

I looked at my brother and the realization hit me like a thunderbolt. I was not delusional. He had said that and he meant it. He held his hand out to me and I backed away. To me, his hand was leprous, diseased with sin. I felt nauseous.

*Absalom will kill you if I tell him this. Whatever happens, I cannot let Absalom know or he'll have your diseased blood on his hands.*

I tried reasoning with Amnon, but there was just no reasoning with a man who had taken leave of his senses and taken a lust-induced trip. He could hear nothing but the dictates of his lust. This lust was his map and his compass. He was destined to go nowhere but to the destination that it dictated or kill himself getting there.

Amnon was stronger than I was. It was impossible for me to stop him once he had determined that he was not about to listen to my pleas for rational behavior. He forced me on to his bed, placed one hand over my mouth, tore at my clothes until I was exposed to him and ravished me. I cried. I kicked. I tossed. It was all to no avail. He was much stronger and so he was able to slake his lust. My protests were ineffectual.

*Lord God, do not let this news come to the ears of my brother Absalom. Send Absalom on a long trip to keep him out of trouble. Let him go to check on his sheep-shearers.*

I prayed this over and over again. There was nothing to be done to save or replace my virtue now, but I wanted my brother Absalom to remain safe. I did not want him to be known as a murderer. Murder would be the only recompense that he would see as just and fitting to mete out to Amnon. Yes, Amnon needed to be punished for the evil that he had done to me, but I did not want Absalom to dish out that punishment. If our father punished him (and I was certain that he would), it would be Godly justice. After all, it is a father's God-given duty to protect his daughter. Yet, I knew that if Absalom got to Amnon before our father did he would kill him and bear the consequences. Absalom was hot-headed like that.

Eventually, Amnon was through. He rolled off me and he sighed with contentment. I could not imagine how such a vile act could bring him such pleasure, but it did. He lay there, satisfied and smug. The stench of his lust exploded from his pores and he inhaled it deeply, seemingly oblivious to the vileness of the sin that he had just committed and of the response that this would draw from our father and from our brother, Absalom. It was as if he had a death wish. I wondered what could have made Amnon suicidal. I moved away from him to the corner of the room. I sat there with my legs pulled up until my thighs touched my chest. I closed my eyes, thinking that if I remained like this long enough I would wake up and this nightmare would vanish from my memory. I dared not leave this place and validate what had just happened. I had been a fool to fall into Amnon's trap and now everyone would know it.

Time crawled by. Amnon fell asleep. He snored the contented snores of a man who was sated. The sound jogged me out of my self-imposed stupor. My desolate life flashed before my eyes. No husband. No children. No servants of my own. The ignominy of having been raped by my brother. Living on someone else's benevolence. My father's subjects would always look at me with pity in their eyes. In one afternoon, all of the dreams that I had nurtured for a lifetime had been taken away and nothing but desolation lay ahead of me like an oasis-less desert. Worse yet, inside my brain, the whispered: **One brother killed the other because of her**.

What started as a whisper echoed in my ears like the bugle call throughout the land when my father was about to make an important proclamation. It boomed against my brain and bounced off my eardrums, resounding ever louder than the preceding whisper until it seemed as if the air in Amnon's chamber was thick with this taunt.

*One brother killed the other because of her.*

*One brother killed the other because of her.*

*One brother killed the other because of her.*

*One brother killed the other because of her.*

*One brother killed the other because of her.*

*One brother killed the other because of her.*

*One brother killed the other because of her.*

*One brother killed the other because of her.*

# *One brother killed the other because of her.*

It was inevitable. Absalom was going to kill him and here he lay, so satisfied with himself. Absalom would never be satisfied to have one of our father's soldiers kill Amnon. He would plead with our father to allow him to be the one to kill him. I doubted that our father would deny him that request.

I began to pray again for Absalom that God would make him see that Amnon's blood ought not to stain his hands. I prayed that the Lord would let me die instead without Absalom having to know what really happened just so that his children would not be tainted by the fact that their father was a murderer. No prayer could undo what Amnon had done to me, so I did not waste time praying for myself. My only concern was Absalom and what he would do when he learnt of this.

I prayed frantically and aloud to block out the sound of Amnon's contented snores and the taunt that rode the waves of that sign of his satisfaction with himself. I prayed and I cried. I did not even realize that Amnon's snores had stopped until I felt his glare burning the skin off my legs and arms and singeing my hair. They were all that he could see as I was still curled up as if not seeing him could erase what had happened. Slowly, I looked up and the hatred that showed so plainly in his eyes burned holes in my chest.

"Arise, be gone."

*Is that all that he is going to say to me? Is his only concern that I leave his quarters? I was right. My brother has taken leave of his senses. He is not responsible for this or for what happened.*

"There is no cause for you to treat me like this, Amnon. This evil in sending me away is greater than the other that you did me."

"I said to arise and go. The sight of you makes me sick. Put on your clothes."

*He is crazy. No! A nagging thought tugged at the edges of my mind until it gained admittance. Slowly, it crossed the plane of my brain: I was being punished for some sin. There could be no other explanation for God allowing this evil to befall me. I have no clue what that sin is,*

*Jehovah, but I wish that you had chosen some other method of punishment. I have tried to do that which is right. I do not know how or when I failed you in such a manner that you have cursed me like this, but I am truly sorry.*

Hatred dripped off Amnon's eyelashes as I got dressed. I feared that it would run across the floor, touch my feet and not just cripple me but turn me into stone. The heat of that hatred made his chamber unbearable. I was glad that I was leaving it though what lay ahead was almost too terrible to think of.

"Manservant, put this woman out from me and bolt the door after her."

*I cannot believe it. He is calling his servant to put me out of his chamber! Is there any cure for madness like this?*

The sunlight brought me to my senses. It was no wild nightmare. It was reality, a harsh reality that would never leave me. No longer was I fit to wear the multi-colored robe that I had worn to Amnon's house. That was reserved for the virgin daughter of the king.

*Where could I go? To Absalom? No!!!! I'd be making him a murderer. To my father? I'll go to my mother. She'll know what I should do.*

The weight of the afternoon's happenings descended on me as I entered my mother's premises. I tore my colored robe and, on my head, placed some ashes that were the remains of a fire that had burnt out nearby. With my hands on my head, I looked up to Heaven and I bawled. I cried for the evil that had repaid my kindness. I cried for the mad man that my brother had become. I cried because I knew deep down that I could not keep my mother's other child unscathed by this evil.

*Lord God of mercy, please allow my mother and I to keep this evil from Absalom. I do not know for sure what the reason for this is, but Lord, please let your wrath end with me. Do not kill our mother with grief. Have mercy on her, O Lord.*

Too late was my prayer. As I approached our mother's quarters, out came Absalom.

"What is the matter with you, Tamar?" Absalom asked as he ushered me into our mother's quarters and away from the prying eyes of others. "Why is your robe torn? Who attacked you?"

He fired the questions at me. Our mother could not even get near me. My inability to answer him as a result of my sobs made him agitated.

"Where has she been?" he demanded of our mother.

Maacah, daughter of Talmai and wife of David, our mother, was at a loss for words. The enormity of the meaning of the torn robe made her speechless and her eyes glassed over with tears. Unlike her daughter, she was able to speak although she knew, like me, what the words that she was about to utter would mean in the life of her son.

"Your father entreated her to tend to her brother Amnon today. Amnon had requested it."

Maacah watched her son as anger raced through his innards and transformed his features just as storm clouds transform the skies. She looked at him look at me and she saw the tears that he controlled. Before he spoke, she noticed also the metamorphosis that he underwent until he almost looked like himself again. She wondered what it meant. She looked deep into his eyes and he looked away to me.

"Has Amnon, your brother, lain with you?"

I could not speak. Words would make this horror more real and confirm the hurt that I saw in their eyes. I nodded. Tears overflowed onto our mother's cheeks.

Those tears formed gouges on my soul. I saw the effect that those tears had on Absalom. He was fighting to keep his teeth together. I could see his jaw twitching.

*How could Amnon do this to my mother? How could he do this to my brother?*

Absalom looked away from both our mother and me for a while. The pain of what had happened weighed his shoulders down. For a brief moment, they actually slumped. He caressed my cheek and our mother moved closer to us.

"We have to do something about this vile act that Amnon has committed. We must let your father know of this thing. He is a just man. He will see to it that Amnon is repaid for his actions as is fair and just. Absalom, let me take your sister in and tend to her bruises. I will get my maidservant to bring her some tea to soothe her shattered nerves. She needs to be cared for. Let me take over here before we take this matter to your father."

Absalom looked at our mother. He looked at me. He shook his head. I knew that he was fighting hard to control his anger. That pained me. He was on the verge of rushing out and killing Amnon. I could feel it in my bones. A new flood of tears poured from my eyes.

Our mother moved closer. I must have been a pitiful sight because she suddenly began to weep uncontrollably as well. Absalom hugged us both. When our mother was able to control herself, Absalom spoke again.

"Hold your peace, my sister. He is your brother. Do not think about this thing. I will speak with our father about this thing that has happened. My mother, I promise you that whatever happens, I will always make provision for my sister."

With that, Absalom left. My mother took me into her inner chamber, took off my clothes and tended to the bruises that until then I had not realized that I had. She got her maidservant to make me some tea and, after she saw to it that I drank it, she put me to bed.

"Sleep, my daughter. Your brother Absalom and I will take care of this. You will be taken care of. We cannot undo this, but we can make sure . . . "

She must have instructed her maidservant to place a sedative in the tea because that was the last thing that I heard her say on the matter.

I fell into a deep sleep, peopled by nightmarish reminders of what Amnon had done to me. I was back in his chambers and he was on top of me, exhaling into my face the putridity of his lust. I tossed about, trying to roll him off. I scratched at his face. I punched at him. All to no avail. When he was satisfied, he laughed in my face: "Get dressed and leave me at once."

"Absalom will kill you," I screamed at him. "Absalom will kill you. He will kill you. He will kill you." And I burst into tears. Even through the tears, I screamed at him. "Absalom will kill you."

"Tamar, Tamar, Tamar."

Through the fog of this nightmare, I could hear my mother calling me. I opened my eyes and she was at my side. She had heard my screams and come to my side. She had taken me into her arms and was rocking me back and forth as she stroked my hair, trying to ease my pain. Tears ran down her cheeks. The sight of those tears made me feel like I could have killed Amnon myself. How could he do this to my mother?

"It is going to be alright, Tamar. Absalom will not kill him. He has gone to talk to your father. Your father will repay

Amnon for his evil deed. Do not fear. Your brother will take care of you. Be calm, my daughter. Rest."

As she continued to rock me and stroke my hair, I drifted back off to sleep.

It was not long before the demon of Amnon's vile act reared its ugly head again. I was soon in the throes of another nightmare and was thrashing about. This time, Amnon was calling: "Manservant, Manservant, come and put this woman out from me." When he saw the shock on my face, he threw his head back and laughed. My response was to pray: "Lord, have mercy on him. He knows what he is doing, but have mercy nonetheless. Lord, let Absalom not get himself in trouble. Let Absalom remember your word that vengeance is yours. Protect Absalom, Jehovah. Protect Absalom. Protect Absalom."

This time, my mother did not call my name. She just took me into her arms and held me against her bosom.

"Jehovah is going to take care of Absalom, Tamar. He is taking care of us all. Absalom is not going to get into any trouble my child."

Again, the tears were trailing down her cheeks. She had been sitting nearby. She had seen me thrashing about and she had heard my prayer and it broke her heart for she knew that Amnon was not going to escape Absalom's wrath if Absalom got to him before our father did.

She got a cool cloth that she had lying nearby and she placed it on my forehead. It was a simple act designed to convey her love and her desire to heal my wounds although she knew that most of my wounds were not physical, but spiritual. She realized that most of my pain was on the inside. I had few bruises on the outside. It was on the inside that I would never be the same again. There was no way to erase the memory of the pain that this incident had brought to my mother and my beloved brother. Little did she or I know when we were thinking this that worse pain was just around the corner.

◆          ◆          ◆

➢ **Absalom speaks with his father**

"Father, excuse this interruption, but I must speak with you about a matter of greatest importance."

♦          ♦          ♦

Absalom had left his mother's quarters with his mind a whirlwind of activity. Yes, he had told his mother and sister that they were to keep this evil quiet and he had given them the impression that he was confident that his father would not allow this evil to go unpunished, but he really did not believe that. Amnon was their father's beloved first born and heir to the throne. He was tempted to go to Amnon's quarters and kill him on the spot. He would not even ask him for an explanation. No explanation could satisfy him so asking Amnon for one would really be pointless.

*I cannot do that. Tamar would die of a broken heart. She did not say it, but her eyes pled with me not to kill him. How could she think of me at this time? My sister is really a gem. How could that wretch do this to her?*

Absalom prayed as he approached his father's receiving area. Although he knew that his father was meeting with some of the elders, he could not wait. He had to hope that when his father found out what this was about that he would forgive this violation of his edict that his family was not to disturb him while he met with the elders. The closer he drew to his father, the more he doubted that his father would be pleased by the disturbance and the less he felt that his father was going to feel that this news could not have waited, but he knew that he had to tell him now.

*Lord God Almighty of Abraham, Isaac and Jacob, please speak to the heart of our father David. Give him the strength of character to deal justly with Amnon so that this evil that Amnon has wrought against my sister Tamar does not go unpaid.*

◆            ◆            ◆

David looked up at his son. He knew that Absalom would not ordinarily defy him and come here frivolously. He saw the emotion on Absalom's face and he feared that someone had died.

"What is it, my son?"

"Father, please forgive my interruption. I need to speak with you alone. I need to speak with you now."

David studied Absalom. He saw the movement of his cheek as he clenched his teeth together. He realized that something terrible had happened in his family. He scanned his memory to see if he had forgotten that someone was slightly ill. He could remember no one other than Amnon and he doubted that Amnon's ailment was the harbinger of death. What then could have brought Absalom here at this time and in this state of agitation? He asked the elders to excuse them. He told them that he had to attend to this matter of his house now. Any man who did not first see to it that all was well in his house, he told them, was not worthy of being head of his household. The elders shuffled out, curious about this thing that had brought Absalom into their midst. He had not been summoned. What could bring him to ask for an urgent audience with his father?

"What is it now, my son?"

"Father, I do not know how to tell you this without bringing you much pain. Amnon has worked a great evil against Tamar. He lay with her."

Shock skipped across the landscape of David's features. It left behind a thick white cloud that made David appear as if he had seen a ghost and he put his hand to his chest as he gasped for air. Absalom feared for his father's life just then.

*Do not tell me that that swine is going to rape my sister and become king of the land in one day. I'll kill him before he ascends the throne.*

Momentarily, David regained his composure. Through clenched teeth, he asked Absalom: "Are you sure of this? Amnon is ill."

David knew that this questioning was only for his own peace of mind. He also knew that Absalom would know that as well. He had no doubt that Absalom would not come to him with such a story if it was not true, but he hated to believe it. Every hair on his body stood on end at the thought of this abomination. He had sent Tamar to tend to Amnon himself. How could Amnon violate his sister in this manner? What repayment for her kindness! The thought of this repugnant act caused anger to course through David's veins and boil his blood. How could Amnon do this? What did he expect him to do? Did he expect him to allow this deed to go unpunished? Could he let this deed go unpunished? Surely Absalom would kill Amnon if he, their father and king of the land, did nothing. What madness had come over Amnon as he lay on his sick bed?

Absalom watched closely as David's thoughts flitted by behind his eyes. He watched and realized that his father was trying to determine how he was going to deal with this without punishing his beloved Amnon. He watched, he realized and he hated his father for his thoughts. It was clear to him then that he had to take care of Amnon himself.

"Tamar is with our mother. Our mother was going to take care of her wounds and put her to bed," Absalom said, having dismissed his father as a viable alternative for Amnon's punishment.

"Is Tamar wounded? How did she get from Amnon's quarters to her mother's? How was Tamar when you left her?" David asked, knowing that Absalom had dismissed him and realizing that he, like Amnon, had incurred Absalom's wrath.

He hoped against hope that this deluge of questions would detract Absalom's attention from the fact that he had not enquired after Tamar before now. He knew his son and he knew that this was not likely, but he had to hope because the alternative thought was too scary: he was commingled with Amnon as the raison d'ètre of Absalom's wrath. He had not come to Tamar's aid as Absalom had wanted him to. He also knew that

Absalom understood fully the reason for his equivocation.

"Tamar did not seem to be suffering much physically. He did not seem to wound her in that way. However, it will be some time before we are able to ascertain truly what damage he did to her spiritually. We all know that she will never marry now. That alone can cause a lot of damage. It is the dream of every woman to be a wife some day. I have already assured our mother that I will make provision for my sister in my house as long as she shall live, but I know that that is a poor substitute for being the mistress of your own household."

"That will not be necessary. She is my daughter. Another of my children has done her wrong. I will continue to make provision for her as is a father's duty."

"No, Father. When you pass on to meet our forefathers, Amnon shall be King. I do not want my sister to be at his mercy. I will provide for her so that when you live no more, she need not have contact with Amnon beyond that which is unavoidable. This thing that he has done her will live with her forever. Let us spare her the agony of living on the alms of the man who deprived her of the privilege of being a wife."

"Your thinking is sound, Absalom."

"I must return to my mother's quarters to see how Tamar is faring. Our mother, as well, will be in need of someone to lift her spirits. This is a very dark day for her too."

"It is a dark day for all of us, Absalom. I am greatly angered by this. Tell your mother that I will be by to see Tamar shortly. I must find this mad man, Amnon, and find out what is going on."

"You need not make any ado about this, Father. I cautioned my mother and sister to be quiet about it as Amnon is your son."

"That is indeed wise. He is my son, but this thing that he has done against my daughter is most vile. Something has to be done about it. Give me some time to think about this and then we shall talk about it again."

David watched his son Absalom go away and he knew that Absalom was not about to allow this vile act of Amnon's to go unpunished. Absalom had spoken of keeping this deed quiet and leaving it to him to deal with Amnon, but David knew that Absalom was not about to allow Amnon to go unpunished for what he had done to Tamar, Absalom's beloved Tamar. Anger welled up in David afresh. How could Amnon do this? Only the God of his forefathers Abraham, Isaac and Jacob could help. He knew that no madness had taken hold of Amnon. He recognized the hand of the God of all life at work. He, David, was being punished for his evil deed. The sins of the father were being visited unto the next generation.

*Father Almighty, have you not punished me enough for the evil that I did to Uriah? First, you took away my child by Bathsheba. Now, you take from me three more children in one fell swoop. Yes, three more children because Absalom is not about to take this as calmly as he would want me to believe. O Lord, that you would strike Amnon yourself rather than have his brother lift his hand against him. Reveal to me what I ought to do in order to protect my son Absalom. There is no undoing Amnon's action. This will always scar Tamar. Please, Lord, show me how to deal with this in such a manner that I do not lose four children to that one sin.*

◆ ◆ ◆

Absalom left his father. He trudged back to his mother's quarters with a heavy heart. This time, his thoughts were really awhirl because he knew beyond a shadow of doubt that his father had no intention of dealing with Amnon as his sin required. He knew that his father's first thoughts had been for Amnon when he heard of the incident. No question about the condition of Tamar until he, Absalom, drew her out from behind the curtain of concern for Amnon and paraded her and all of her vulnerability before their father. His father's barrage of questions about her condition did not fool him. Not a question about how their mother was holding up in the midst of this adversity and she was his wife. She was not just a concubine. All of his father's concern was for the criminal: Amnon. There was no avoiding it. Dealing with Amnon was left to him in spite of the further pain that this was going to cause Tamar.

Again he prayed.

*Lord God Almighty, I beseech you to deal mercifully with my sister Tamar. I am obliged to exact revenge from Amnon since our father is too weak to do so. Jehovah, allow me to do this thing without any harm to my body that I may one day return to the land that you have given to us and take care of my family. Bring peace to the hearts of Tamar and our mother, Maacah, while I am away. Bring peace to them, Almighty God, I beseech you. Amen.*

◆          ◆          ◆

### ➤ **Vengeance**

Two years passed. I lived in Absalom's house, cherished by my brother. He felt guilty. He bore a guilt that he need not feel. He could not command our father to punish Amnon for what he had done. The sight of Amnon going about the land, beloved heir to the throne burned holes into Absalom's heart. I was burdened by this hurt that my brother felt. I tried my best to ease his pain. Whenever possible, I made sure to bring some small joy to my brother's life.

I have come a long way from where Amnon's actions left me that fateful day two years ago. I have come through many a struggle to arrive here. The path here had been populated by nightmares and periods of depression coupled with the pain of seeing my mother pine away to a mere shadow of her former self and my brother struggle to keep himself from being a murderer.

At first, I was consumed by hatred. I hated Amnon for what he had taken away from me. I hated our father because, while he came by and demonstrated a measure of concern, it was evident that he was more concerned with Amnon. He had done nothing to punish him. That hurt. I hated the people who lowered their eyes rather than look me in the face. Their pity was tangible, so thick between us that I would need a spear to pierce it if I hoped to see the other side. At those times, I hated Amnon even more. My hatred was a palpable wall between me and the people around me. I did not speak unless I was first addressed and I could not avoid returning an answer. I never sought the company of others. I would sit in the dark if I was allowed to. The hatred festered, creating gangrene in my soul, changing me from the child of sunlight and love that my mother and brother so cherished to a gnarled caricature of my former self. I saw the pained look that my hatred-guarded imprisonment caused my mother and brother. I realized that if I was able to break free of the tyranny of hatred, I would be able to return to my former self and bring them the joy that they so desperately sought. But I could not. There seemed to be no escaping from the solitary confinement of hatred.

Then, one day, I saw Amnon pass by. He strutted by with his head high in the air and the look on his face boasted of absolute calm. His manner told the world that he would one day be king and he had not a care in the world. No mention of the fact that he was a rapist. Not a murmur about the atrocious deed that he had committed just two years before. At that point, I realized that I was punishing myself as Amnon should have been punished. Instead of him feeling the weight of his heinous crime, I was bearing its crippling weight on my back. That moment was a turning point in my life. No more was I going from day to day with this excrescent hatred sitting with all of its camel-weight on my chest, boring holes in my intestines, poisoning the life-blood that was running in my veins and eating away at my brain cells. It was a parasite keeping its host just short of dead, just alive enough to provide it the sustenance that it needed for survival. There was only one way that I knew to overcome the seemingly impossible: the Lord God Almighty. I began to pray immediately.

*Lord God Almighty, you who provided my father, David, the strength to defeat Goliath, I, your much-wronged daughter, come to you in supplication. You know the circumstances that brought me to this place. You also know that you alone can bring about a change in my life. I cannot live like this any longer. Like my forefather, Jacob who refused to let go of your messenger, I am not letting go at this time. Jehovah, look upon me with mercy. I cannot continue like this. I am being eaten alive by this hatred. I need sweet release or I will surely die. I am not asking you to visit any punishment on Amnon. I am only asking that you free me from this all-consuming hatred. Amen.*

I prayed and I cried. I cried and I prayed some more. I prayed for hours. When my brother Absalom found me, it was dark and I was weak from the weight of my prayers and my tears. Absalom was greatly concerned by the state that I was in.

"What is the matter, sister? Tell me," he coaxed.

I could not tell him. I could not let him know that I was still reaping the crop of that hateful seed sown by Amnon. I looked at him and the tears ran down my cheeks. My lips were sealed by fear.

"Talk to me, Tamar," he said as he rubbed my hands between his. Concern dripped from his every pore, yet I could not tell him.

"Do not be afraid to tell me. Did someone do you some evil? Are you feeling sick?"

I shook my head as negative response to his inquiries.

For a while, he sat there, rubbing my hands between his. A puzzled look remained on his face then he asked, "Are you still bothered by what Amnon did?"

My lips trembled. "Yes," was my whispered response. I wanted to say so much more, but couldn't.

I looked at the clenching and unclenching of Absalom's jaw and knew that it would not be long before Amnon was no more. I knew that Absalom would not allow him to strut about much more while I remained in pain.

"Tell me about it. How do you feel, Tamar? Do you hate him?"

My tears dried immediately. The shock of his insight was potent enough to turn the faucet of my tears off without any dripping.

"I did, but then I saw him pass by today and I realized that while his sin weighed heavily on my chest, it was forgotten by him. Now, I know that for me to hate him or our father is pointless."

"My sister, I want you to know that in due course, Amnon's payment is going to come to him and he is going to recognize it for what it is and be unable to avoid it."

"Absalom, I do not want you to get yourself in trouble over Amnon. He is not worth it."

"My sister, I will try not to bring you and our mother any grief, but if I am the tool that the Lord, who repays all evil deeds, is going to use to punish Amnon for what he has done to you, then, so be it."

"Absalom . . ."

"My sister, Tamar, you need not worry. You will be taken care of and there is no stopping the will of the Lord. Anyway, I was looking for you to let you know that I will be going to join my sheep-shearers in Baalhazor tomorrow. I know that you worry when I am away, but I wanted to let you know that I will not be away any longer than necessary. Whatever happens,

I'll be back as soon as possible, so take care of our mother and yourself as usual."

"Take care of yourself, Absalom."

We hugged and he left to take care of some other matters. I did not see him the next morning before he left.

◆　　　　◆　　　　◆

I could hear my blood thundering through my veins and my heart pounding as if to escape from my chest. I placed my hands on my head and I bawled like everyone else in my brother's house seemed to be doing at that moment. The din was maddening. The compound reverberated with the sounds of our grief.

*Lord, how could you let this happen? Do you hate me so much? Do you not care about my mother? Who do you really intend to punish? My father? If so, could you not have found some other method? Could you be so intent on punishing my father that you do not care about the others of us who would bear the brunt of this grief?*

I could not believe this thing that I was hearing. Absalom had killed Amnon! Why had Amnon gone to where Absalom and his sheep-shearers were? Amnon had no sheep-shearers and he had never shown any interest in what Absalom's sheep-shearers were doing before now. The news swam about in what seemed to be a vacuum where my brain used to be in residence. I seemed incapable of a single, coherent thought. They all seemed to run together.

*What was I going to tell my mother? Where had Absalom gone? The person who brought the news had said, but I cannot remember. Was it that the person had said that Absalom was dead and I was refusing to believe it?*

I washed my face and left my quarters in my brother's house to find my mother. She was sitting within her house with ashes on her head. She must have heard. She looked up through her veil of tears as I came in.

"Tamar, my child," was all that she got out before she was awash with tears again.

I tried to comfort her. I rocked her as she had rocked me two years before. I stroked her hair as she had done mine. I sent her maidservant to get her some tea as she had done then. I called for a cold rag to place on her forehead, just as she had. I tried everything that I could think of, but my mother seemed inconsolable. She tried to speak.

"I heard the news, Mother. You do not need to speak."

"Tamar, I have to tell you. Absalom did not just fall on Amnon and kill him in the heat of the moment. He planned it and he planned it well. Amnon must have known before he died that this was Absalom's revenge for what he had done to you . . . "

"What do you mean, Mother?"

Absalom's words to me the night before he left, rang in my ears and my blood took an icy course through my veins on its way to my heart where I feared that it would puncture it and kill me.

"*. . . Amnon's payment is going to come to him and he is going to recognize it for what it is and be unable to avoid it.*"

"Amnon knew that Absalom had asked your father to allow him to accompany him just as Amnon had asked your father to allow you to attend to him when he was pretending to be sick. Amnon must also have realized that Absalom had planned this just as Amnon had planned his attack on you because the report says that Absalom only had to tell his men to smite Amnon and they killed him right away."

"Did you hear any report about what has become of Absalom? Do you know where he is now?"

"My father, Talmai, King of Geshur, sent a messenger to let me know that Absalom is in Geshur and safe. His servant arrived at the same time as your father's."

"My father's servant? Does my father know where Absalom is?"

"Your father sent a servant to let me know what Absalom had done. He did not say if your father knows where Absalom is, but I doubt that he does."

Only then did I have any thought of how my father would be affected by this happening. I felt guilty that I had not thought of him before.

"Did he say how my father is?"

"Your father is deeply saddened by this. His exact words were that your father 'wept a great deal'."

"Mother, you need to get a rest. Absalom will be taken care of by your father in the land of Geshur. We need to take care of ourselves until he returns for he shall be back. I must see how my father is doing. He has lost two sons today."

"Tamar, you are a blessing, more so now than when you were a baby, all rosy and full of smiles. You think of your father at this time even though he has treated you so unfairly while he thought only of his beloved son Amnon. Your father is king, yet he could not act in a kingly or fatherly fashion. Your brother Absalom was obliged to kill Amnon to avenge that vile act that Amnon committed against you. I hope that your father knows that the Lord has blessed him with a wonderful daughter."

"Mother, Amnon did me a great wrong and my father, great man though he is, was unable to deal with Amnon as he should have. The wrong that is perceived that he did to me, he did to himself because he has now lost his beloved firstborn son as a result of a sin that he let go unpunished. He was satisfied to have me condemned to a life as a desolate woman, living in my brother's house, but I am no longer desolate. Hatred would have kept me desolate, but I was set free from the bonds of hatred before Amnon was killed. Now, my father will experience what it is to be desolate as he mourns the loss of not one son but two. I hope that one day, he too can be released from his desolate state by the same one who set me free: Jehovah Shalom, our God who gives peace."

With those few words, Tamar set off in search of her father: a once-desolate woman bringing hope and joy and peace to the heart of a now-desolate man.